AMINA MAKING OF A QUEEN

Sholape Kolawole

Book Title Copyright © 2018 by Sholape Kolawole. All Rights Reserved.

All rights reserved. No part of this book may be reproduced in any form or by any electronic or mechanical means including information storage and retrieval systems, without permission in writing from the author. The only exception is by a reviewer, who may quote short excerpts in a review.

Cover designed by Martin CS.

Maps illustration by Samia Javed.

While inspired by real events and historical characters, this book is a work of fiction, and does not claim to be historically accurate or portray factual events or relationships. Names, characters, places, and incidents may not be factually accurate.

Sholape Kolawole

Visit my website at www.sholapekolawole.com

Printed in the United States of America

First Printing: 2018

ISBN-13: 978-1-7328998-1-0

*To my wife, Toyin Kolawole, and
my wonderful boys, Feolu and Simi Kolawole.
You are my joy, my love, and the light of my world.
Thank you for believing in me.*

Sixteenth Century Africa - Hausaland, Nupeland, and Songhai

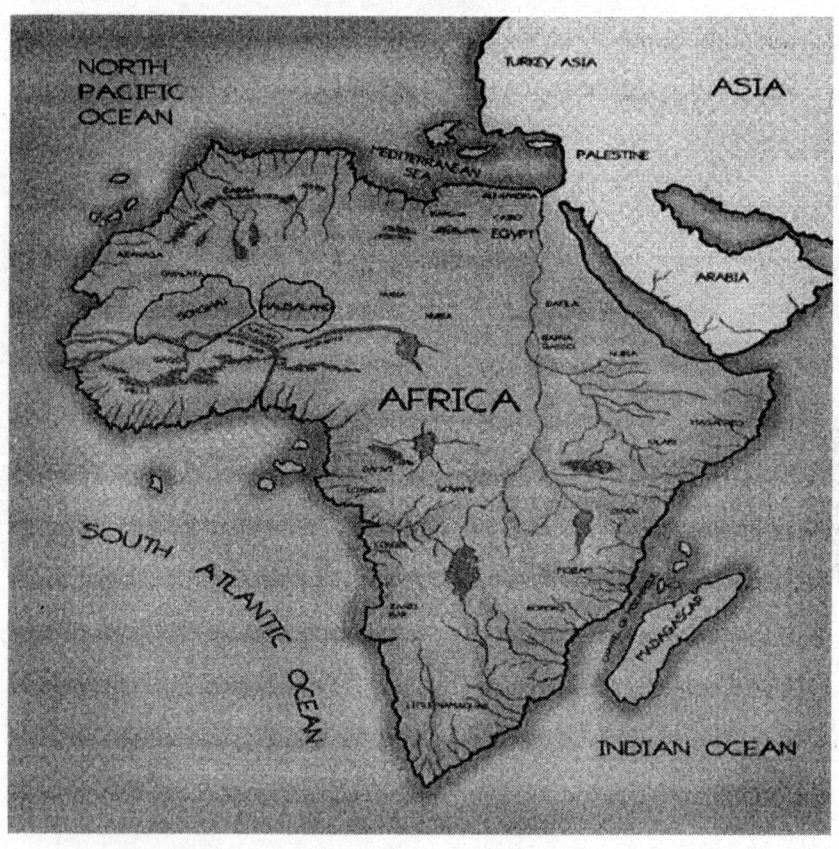

Sixteenth century Africa - a continent of abundant culture, resources, and varied civilizations. Songhai empire to the west, and Nupeland south of Hausaland, pose the greatest threats to the Hausaland region. These empires are seeking to expand into Hausaland, to gain control of the illustrious trade routes of Cairo and Mecca.

Sixteenth Century West Africa Villages - Hausaland and Nupeland

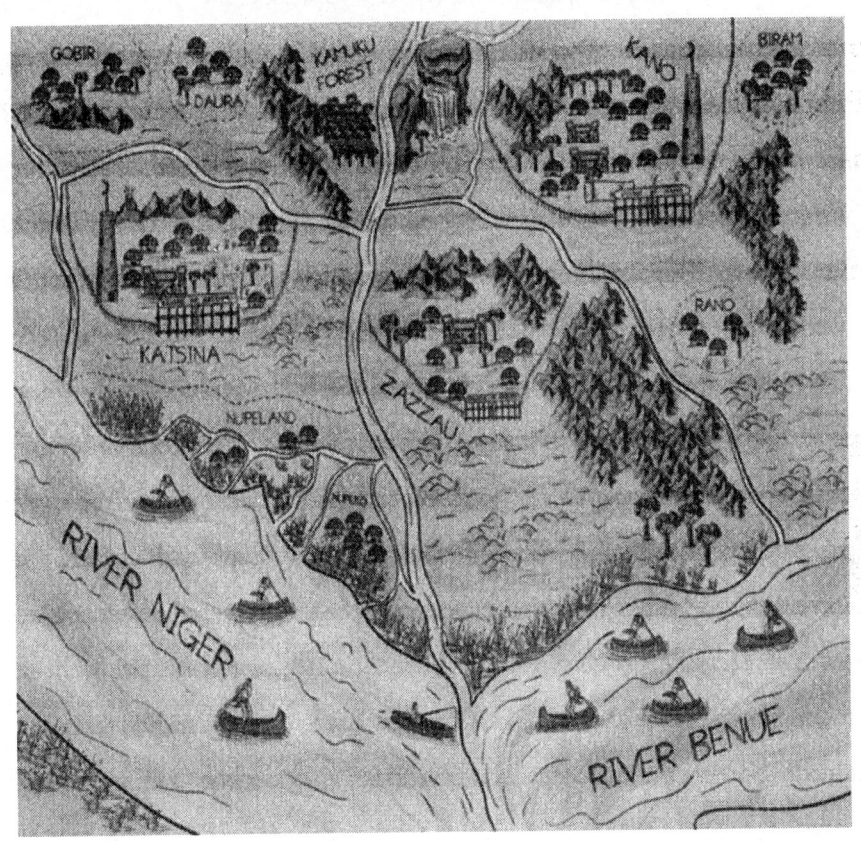

Sixteenth century West Africa, the seven villages of Hausaland - Zazzau, Rano, Kano, Biram, Katsina, Daura, and Gobir, exist as distinct entities. Zazzau, because of its proximity to Nupeland in the south, is most susceptible to Nupe incursion...

A TYRANT'S INVASION

A DESTINY IN MOTION

A WARRIOR PRINCESS WILL
ARISE TO BE GREATER THAN
ANY MAN

CHAPTER ONE

Amina – Curious and Fearless

Curiosity without bravery is like a dog that cannot bark

Early Harmattan Season. Late 1546

AMINA CLIMBED SLOWLY UPWARDS towards the crest of a sandy hill to her favorite hiding spot behind a stunted tree trunk. The musty smell of Harmattan winds tinged with faint droplets of rain wafted through her nostrils. She felt the soft breeze caress her bare, brown shoulders.

In the distant horizon, she observed the setting sun cast a dull orange glow across the sky, and over the vast settlement of clay huts and mud fences that was her beloved homeland – the Hausa tribal village of Zazzau. Amina studied the sky with inquisitive eyes, hopeful that the smell of rain in the air was not a warning of an imminent downpour. Indeed, it was but a tease. The rainy season was gone for now, swept away by the Saharan Harmattan. The moisture in the air was the dying breath of a season ending; a reminder of what was to once again return after the dry Harmattan had run its season long course.

Amina had climbed up the hill stealthily, like a Cheetah stalking its prey in the wild grasslands of the Kamuku forest northwest of her homeland. The last thing she wanted was to be discovered and sent back home before she had a chance to view the spectacle of the Sojojin Zazzau - Zazzau's warriors, training in the valley below.

It was what she had come all this way for. Now, she had reached her favorite spot and was trying to settle in. She had curled up quite easily behind the tree trunk when she was little. But that was a long time ago. By the counting of the Harmattan and Rain seasons past, Amina was now a young woman – sixteen years of age. Her legs were getting way too long to tuck away in that cramped spot.

I need to find a new hiding place, thought Amina, staring down at her long, brown leg as it barely curled under her lithe figure. She was increasingly conscious of her rapidly maturing body. She hated the changes. But her body was well into its transformation. She could hear her mother now as clearly as the first day she had experienced the pain – the pain that is normal for women of childbearing age.

"Aminatu, my daughter," her mother had begun softly, calling her full name as she typically would when chastising her. *"Yi Ha'kuri fa.* Our people say bucking will not permanently free a donkey from its load because the donkey's owner, will simply put the load on its back again. It is a woman's duty to bear children. So, you must embrace this change and thank our ancestors of counting you worthy of fertility."

Amina pouted her full lips and spat on the dusty earth as she recalled those words. She detested the widely accepted tradition that a woman's duty was to produce offspring and tend the family while the man, on the other hand, was revered as the powerful protector and decision maker of the family and village.

She had observed and concluded that men were cowards who liked nothing more than to eat kola nuts and bask on shaded wooden benches away from the noonday sun. There, under sleep's spell, they would drool endlessly, nodding away now and again like the orange-necked lizards that idled away on the dusty paths and weather worn trees of Zazzau.

She glanced at her royal silk veil which she had folded and tucked into the side of the short, leather loincloth she wore around her waist. She drew satisfaction in the fact that she was choosing not to hide her looks behind the veil anymore.

In the valley below, a man stood on the sideline, barking orders as loudly as he could to a myriad of fatigued warriors dressed in official battle uniform. The uniform ensemble included a knee-length leather dashiki made of tough elephant hide, a leopard skin waist belt, baggy leather pants that ended in a tight wrap around the ankles, and snake-skin sandals.

The man on the sideline was a tall burly man with arms the size of massive yam tubers and a shiny, shaved head. He was a stern man. He had a frown like a battle scar etched in his features to prove it. This man was Madaki Zaki. For the past ten seasons, he was the supreme commander of the Sojojin Zazzau.

Amina saw Madaki Zaki look up at the setting sun. Day's training would need to end soon. Then she heard a piercing scream. She jerked her head up, glancing around her and across to the hill opposite her. There appeared to be a deep contour at the crest of the opposite hill. Her eyes widened in horror.

As Madaki Zaki looked up, he also heard the piercing scream. The scream was unmistakably from a distressed female. The Sojojin Zazzau, engaged in a variety of training activities such as sword fighting, archery, javelin throwing and physical combat, paused as the shrill cry shattered the evening's serenity.

Madaki Zaki looked across at the hillcrests on either side of the valley, searching for the origin of the cry. He glanced inquiringly at his assistant commander, Ahmed, a comparatively smaller but nonetheless imposing man, who stood next to him.

Ahmed gave his leader a nonplussed look and shrugged his shoulders. Madaki Zaki knew he had to investigate. He ordered the men to resume training and asked Ahmed to briefly take over command.

"Shall I ask some warriors to accompany you sir?" Ahmed asked, almost mechanically starting to search for recruits to go with Madaki Zaki.

Madaki Zaki shook his head vehemently, already moving towards the hills. Why would he who had single-handedly battled a lion need help to go investigate why a woman might be in distress? "No need," he said.

There was a man, and a young girl on the hillcrest. The girl was struggling to free herself from his powerful grip. But it was no use. He was too strong. He was forcing himself on her, clasping one hand over her mouth to muffle her screams.

Amina's anger rose like hot balls of coal. How beastly could a man be? She was afraid for the young girl. What if he killed her? Her mind was racing.

Perhaps she could get over there. Maybe she could somehow distract him long enough for the girl to get away. But how would she get there? She could climb all the way down the hill, circle around the valley, and climb up the opposite hill. But that would take quite some time, and that would give the wicked man too much time to complete his act.

Amina pondered for a few moments, her agitation brimming like water in an earthen pot over flaming wood. She then searched around her for a rock that could fit in her hand and quickly found one. She grabbed it, rose, and took several steps back. Then, she hurled the rock with all her might in the direction of the opposite hill.

She crouched to keep from being detected if her stone had alerted the wicked man. She waited, her heartbeat thundering away like a chariot of horses. The rock had barely reached the other side.

What if she failed to make it to the other side? The valley below was deep enough that she would get hurt, or worse.

Amina listened. All was quiet, but she could still hear that piercing scream reverberating in her soul. She imagined the wicked man forcing himself onto the girl. She needed to help, she had to help.

She shut her eyes and slowed her breath. Breathing in and out, she counted each breath to calm her nerves. Do not think, just do, she thought to herself. Eyes still closed, she rose, and took several steps back. She then paused for a moment and took several additional steps back. She memorized how many steps she took. She would recount those steps, albeit at a faster pace, when she made her run.

In her mind's eye, Amina saw her safe landing on the opposite hill. She listened for the wind. She was counting on it to help propel her. She steadied her breath, tensing her muscles until all felt still around her.

Then, her eyes flew open and she bolted like a maddened cheetah towards the cliff of the hill. She felt the wind all around and she harnessed its force, her mind focused on her jump off point.

When she reached the edge, she thrust herself forward with all her might, and propelled herself forward with wild, cycling but coordinated motions of her arms and legs.

For a while Amina felt the wind propel her as she had hoped. Her short braids flapped in the wind, and her cycling arms and legs helped to thrust her forward. She could see the cliff of her target fast approaching when she realized she had not contemplated how she would land. Even if she made it across safely, she could get hurt if she landed awkwardly. She panicked in that instant, lost coordination and immediately began to lose elevation. She was falling.

Amina bit her lower lip to keep from crying out in fear. She tasted blood. Panic-stricken, she tried to regain her cycling motion, but her coordination was gone, and arms and legs were now flailing.

She squeezed her eyes shut and braced for a fall to the valley below. Her entire body suddenly felt heavy like a log and her heart seemed to have frozen inside her chest. Her terrified eyes flew open almost as soon as she shut them, looking to see where she might meet her demise.

She was lucky. She saw that she was about to land quite awkwardly atop the sandy plain of her destined hill. She folded her legs below her just in time to forestall an awkward landing. She landed on her waist and backside. She groaned in pain, forcing herself to roll several times to quell the heavy impact of her fall.

When her last roll was completed, Amina lay in a heap covered in dust, her face buried in the sandy hilltop. Her entire body heaved as though the earth beneath her was undulating.

Now she felt her frozen heart thawed. It pounded against her ribcage like a wild, angry bull trapped in a pen. The magnitude of her feat dawned on her and she could scarcely believe it. Exhilaration and urgency swept through her at once and lifted her up. She groaned again in pain and looked up to behold the face of the wicked man.

The wicked man looked ordinary enough, cowardly even, as his eyes darted about. His eyes bulged with shock and fear at what he had just witnessed – the young girl before him leaping over the valley.

He drew a small dagger from his baggy cotton pants and thrust it in Amina's direction.

"Be gone from here at once, or I will surely slit your throat," he growled, deepening his voice to mask the fear that threatened to overwhelm him.

Amina looked at the dagger he brandished, and at his other hand which firmly gripped the hair of the crying girl as though she was a rag doll.

The girl, barely able to cover her naked body, began to struggle to break free. She cried out with petrified, pleading eyes fixed on Amina. "Help me, please! Please, please help me."

"Silence!" the wicked man roared, gaining confidence with each passing moment. He gripped her hair so tight that it spurted blood at its roots. The girl cried out in pain and cowered.

"I said leave. Now!" he growled again thrusting the dagger towards Amina and clenching his teeth to appear menacing. As he did so, his face suddenly drained of all menace and his lips began to tremble with fear.

At first glance, this young girl appeared clothed like any other in a simple leather loincloth made of antelope skin and sandals of similar material. The dyed cotton wrapper she wore across her chest was equally simple.

But as the wicked man examined her further, his lust-crazed mind cleared, and he began to realize the defiant girl covered in dust before him must be important.

Her clothing was simple, but her beautification was elaborate. She was adorned in gold rings – markings of her royal heritage. Two gold rings hung from either side of her navel. Multiple, skin-tight gold bracelets shone on her wrists and upper arms. Gold anklets gleamed on her ankles, and large bronze earrings added a rich dimension to her youthful, natural beauty.

"Who are..."

The wicked man's words died in his mouth as a bolder voice behind him finished his sentence and a strong hand forcibly yanked the dagger from his hand.

"She whom you have threatened is Amina, granddaughter of our beloved ruler of Zazzau, Habe Nohi."

The wicked man spun around, crashing to his knees at the sight of Madaki Zaki's imposing figure and began to plead for mercy as he released his captive. Amina was always veiled at public functions. He would never have recognized her, he explained apologetically.

The young girl rushed to Amina and flung her arms around her waist, almost knocking her down in the process. She hugged Amina as tightly as she could, sobbing and thanking her.

Amina, drained of all fight and fervor, was initially taken aback by the girl's emotional gratitude. But then she returned the embrace and began rocking the sobbing girl like a mother would to a child.

Amina breathed a deep sigh of relief and cast her eyes on the kneeling figure of the wicked man and Madaki Zaki standing with arms akimbo before him. She had not stopped to think of the danger she had put herself in to save this girl until now. She had never been happier to see Madaki Zaki.

Amina recognized the wicked man as a Zazzau village lowlife who spent his days either begging in the streets or plotting how to steal from the unwitting. She only recognized him because he had been punished for theft and banditry in the past.

"Mustapha, you despicable dog," Madaki Zaki began. "I will hand you over to my warriors who will bind you by your arms and legs like the animal that you are and take you back to the village to stand trial before the Habe and his council of nobles."

As Madaki Zaki uttered the words, Mustapha crashed his forehead to ground and cried out louder for mercy. Overcome by a tremendous fear of the fate that might befall him if he was arraigned before the Habe, he rushed to kiss Madaki Zaki's feet and to pledge himself to slavery. He begged Madaki Zaki to consider that Habe Nohi would not be merciful.

Madaki Zaki kicked the onrushing Mustapha hard in the temple before he reached his destination. The kick sent Mustapha to the ground. His body collapsed before Madaki Zaki like a broken tree branch struck by a storm. Madaki Zaki spat on the unconscious body and kicked him again in the ribcage. Then he turned to address Amina.

He glared at Amina with arms folded across his chest. His dashiki uniform, unlike that of his warriors, was sleeveless, as though his yam-tuber biceps could not be contained by sleeves. He furrowed his thick eyebrows and scowled.

Amina rocked the young girl while looking in a petitioning manner from Madaki Zaki to the girl and back to Madaki Zaki. She broke into a sheepish, disarming smile.

Yes, she had stolen away from the village to watch the Sojojin Zazzau train and sure, that leap was beyond dangerous. She still wasn't sure how she had managed it.

But surely, Madaki Zaki would choose to accept above it all that she had done something good here. What if she had not been here? Something terrible would have happened to this young girl. "Princess Amina!" Madaki Zaki began. His deep voice was stern, reprimanding.

"*Ranka ya dade* Madaki Zaki!" Amina sheepishly offered.

Madaki Zaki remained stoic for a moment, unmoved by her exaggerated show of respect.

"*Kai* Amina, my young princess! I saw you leap over the valley. That was an impossible jump *fa. Ko ba haka ba?* Why would you ever try something so dangerous? You could have been killed! And what would your mother say if she knew you were out here alone?"

The young girl had calmed down and now ventured to appeal on Amina's behalf.

"Madaki Zaki, please don't blame her. But for her, I might be dead. I have no words to express the depth of gratitude I feel towards her for risking her noble life to save that of a peasant."

Madaki Zaki observed the girl, appearing to consider her appeal. When he finally spoke, it was with some concern and empathy. "What is your name, young girl? And who are your parents? Are you hurt in any way?"

"My name is Aisha. My father is Idris, a carpenter. My mother is Laila. We live in the southeast corridor of the village," she said.

Aisha looked down at her toes, embarrassed as she pulled her ripped wrapper tighter across her chest. She choked as she continued, fresh tears streaming down her face.

"I am not hurt. I thank our ancestors that Princess Amina appeared just in time. He was about to..." her voice trailed off.

Amina hugged and consoled Aisha. She threw Madaki Zaki a triumphant I-told-you-so look. She wanted to ask Aisha how it was that she came to be out here alone with Mustapha but decided it was not important at this time. She was happy Aisha was unhurt and that was enough.

More importantly, she was reluctant to provide Madaki Zaki with an opportunity to ask the same question of her.

Madaki Zaki had said to her, on many occasions, that it was customary for boys to be brave and girls to be protected – a custom as precious as cow dung in Amina's opinion. But now would be an inopportune time to engage Madaki Zaki in a debate about the merits of the belief.

"Very well, we shall return to the palace at once," Madaki Zaki finally announced. "It is getting quite late. My warriors will bring this Mustapha imbecile back to the village when they complete their training. He will pay for his crime, Aisha, you can be certain of that, ok?"

Aisha nodded silently.

"Princess Amina, you will ride with me on my horse. Aisha, I will designate a trusted warrior with whom you will ride."

Amina observed the sun in sluggish descent as she mounted the saddle behind Madaki Zaki for the home journey. She wondered which family member the supreme commander would deliver her to.

She hoped that his fondness for her would influence a decision to deliver her to grandfather, not Mama. Mama would make more of it than was necessary, like she always did.

The horseback ride back to the palace was short but refreshing against the waves of the seasonally cool Harmattan winds. Amina felt the wind whip across her face and between the thin strips of bare skin on her head, exposed by her hair braids.

She wrapped her slender arms tightly around Madaki Zaki's ribcage and leaned into him, feeling the strength exuded by his upper body as his horse galloped towards Zazzau.

Soon, the bamboo stick fence that surrounded the entire Zazzau village began to emerge. The fence, built for security, was the height of two full grown Zazzau men and was well fortified with countless, horizontally-protruding bamboo spears. The entrance to the village was sealed with huge metal gates with the words Village of Zazzau inscribed at the top.

As Madaki Zaki's horse sprinted over an elevated part of the vast, dusty terrain that surrounded Zazzau, Amina observed the vast settlement of clay huts inside her village as far as she could see.

She saw the wide village square in the center, demarcated from the east and west villager dwelling corridors by a stone wall. Behind the village square and in front of the south villager dwelling corridor was the palace courtyard.

She noted the white stucco walls and thatched ceilings of several mudbrick dwellings within the palace courtyard. These were the dwellings of the royal family and their servants. The elegant dwellings were easy to spot as they were multi-storied with the upper level stories having balcony style parapet walls.

The building fronts were plastered in white stucco and decorated with vivid abstract art of Zazzau battle conquests. She couldn't see, but recalled from memory, the surroundings of the courtyard.

The dry mud walls were beautified with hanging plants and dried animal skins. The courtyard was lined with wooden sculptures of the twelve Habes who had ruled Zazzau before her grandfather.

Amina considered what her mother would be doing at that moment – likely catering to the whims of her lazy father, Nikitau. Amina hissed at the thought of her father. She did, for a moment as they neared Zazzau, worry that Madaki Zaki might hand her over to her mother who, she was certain, would punish her and then never cease nagging about her misadventure.

But she took comfort in the knowledge that Madaki Zaki was more unlikely to do such. He was, after all, the one who had encouraged her, since she was a little girl, to take a keen interest in Zazzau's history and military conquests.

Amina imagined her father, Nikitau, waiting to be served supper as he lazily drank Burukutu from that coursed wooden gourd while chewing noisily on red kola nuts.

He would likely be seated on a wooden bench on the balcony of his mudbrick dwelling or outside the lower floor of the dwelling within the expansive palace courtyard, dressed in a white vest and a purple loincloth.

Purple was Zazzau's royal color – no one outside the royal family was permitted even a sliver of purple in their attire. Amina did not think her father deserved to attire in purple. She shook her head to dispel the mental image of his lazy sprawl.

Amina pressed harder into Madaki Zaki's muscular body and shut her eyes, grateful that Zazzau had courageous warriors like him to keep the people safe. She briefly remembered Madaki Zaki's legend: how he killed a lion, from the Kamuku forest, that preyed on the people of Zazzau. Perhaps she also would do something great for Zazzau someday.

The sentry on guard in the mud-walled post overlooking Zazzau's gates recognized Madaki Zaki on horseback from a distance. He instructed the two guards down below to open the massive metal gates for the approaching supreme commander.

CHAPTER TWO

Nupe – An Imminent Threat

A wise man is cautious about everything, even his shadow

HABE NOHI WAS BUSY adjudicating a village dispute when Madaki Zaki arrived at the palace with Amina in tow. Before Habe Nohi, a young woman knelt, paying homage. Beside this woman, a male companion, not much older than she was, knelt as well with his head bowed in reverence.

A third villager also stooped with one knee down and his head bowed. This villager was older than the pair, as evidenced by his graying hair.

Habe Nohi shifted to a comfortable position on his throne. The cotton-padded majestic throne was positioned at the far end of his palace. Giant bronze lion sculptures lay beside each arm. The throne was flanked by several hefty, bare-chested guards armed with gleaming machetes. It was ornamented with golden orbs, gems, and shiny gold stones purchased from Gao tradesmen who traversed the Senegal river.

Habe Nohi briefly studied the silent trio before lifting his head to observe all others in the palace. The multi-storied palace was intentionally situated at the far end of the palace courtyard. The distance provided ample consideration time for anyone bringing a disputed matter to the Habe.

Habe Nohi hoped each disagreeing party before him had carefully considered the merits of their case. He would render swift judgment on the guilty party.

He observed, before him, his noble council members on wooden stools: Alkatin Aliyu, the wiry old chief judge, Wali Sani, the youthful, scholarly chief lawmaker, Lawan Shehu, the ever-attentive village head, and Amina's father, Nikitau who was numbered with the esteemed council solely because of his marriage to Princess Bakwa, the Habe's daughter.

The only member of the council who was absent was Madaki Zaki who had been excused to train the Zazzau warriors in the training valley.

Sani, a bald palace clerk, stood at attention beside one of the hefty guards. He was nowhere near as menacing as the guards. Sani was short, and potbellied, with flabby arms that appeared like deflated balloons compared to the robust muscles of the able-bodied guards beside him.

But, Sani was just as dedicated and conscientious as the other guards. He adopted a classic military stance. His chest jutted out with hairs that were thick and tangled like a bird's nest. His arms hung loosely by his sides and his face was focused forward with eyes rarely blinking.

Habe Nohi gave a nod to Sani who then promptly narrated, without empathy or emotion, the facts of the case precisely as they had been described to him by the parties seeking resolution.

The young woman, Binta, was accused of theft. She was accused of stealing two yams from the older man's storage hut. Binta appeared heartbroken by this accusation. She was in tears – her beautiful, young face as wet as the faces of playful children dipping in the streams of Zazzau during the new yam festival celebration.

But unlike those children, Binta felt no joy now. She vehemently denied the accusation, insisting instead that her brother, kneeling next to her, had gifted her the two yams from the plentiful harvest in his own storage hut.

When Sani concluded, Habe Nohi shifted again on his throne, thoughtfully rubbing his jaw just above the base of the turban that wrapped around his beard. The base of his turban rested in folds on his embroidered babban riga— a floor-length blanket-like robe with long, wide sleeves folded to expose his hands.

Habe Nohi's appearance was noble and somewhat mysterious, with face half-hidden behind the traditional purple turban which covered his head, forehead, and chin.

His brows were creased in deep thought as he cast his eyes through the open palace doors to the palace courtyard outside, seemingly willing the beautiful courtyard to aid his judgment.

At the center of the courtyard, an elevated concrete landing stood, atop of which was a life-sized wooden sculpture of himself. The sculpture stood tall and astride, holding a flaming torch in one outstretched hand and an unsheathed sword in the other.

The torch was a symbol of the Habe as the guiding light and able protector of the Zazzau people. Habe Nohi mused over the role he was being asked to play now – the guiding light role.

The inner palace walls were decorated with animal skins and hanging plants. Bronze Kakati - long trumpets that were considered the emblem of rulers in Hausaland – were displayed on all walls.

Habe Nohi returned his gaze to the trio before him. Binta's husband, Adamu, was fat and lazy. Everyone knew that. He hated farming and could barely provide enough for himself and Binta to eat, so it was plausible that Binta was desperate for food.

Adamu was not being accused of a crime and therefore, was not summoned before the Habe. It seemed a stretch to think that a young woman like Binta could have single-handedly orchestrated such a theft.

Habe Nohi had been informed that Elder Musa, the older man, had a thatched fence around his compound and a small metal gate like most villagers did. So how would Binta have gained access to his yams if acting on her own?

And even if she did develop an elaborate maneuver to gain access to his compound, why would she? She had a very able and prosperous brother who was more than willing to assist in a thieving scheme to feed his sister.

Habe Nohi leaned forward to address Binta's brother.

"Abu, *Fada gaskiya*...is it true what your sister has said?"

"*Ranka ya dade*, Habe Nohi," Abu began, with his right hand raised at elbow length in customary salutation.

"May you live long and may generations to come tell of your greatness, your unmatched wisdom, and your heart of pure gold. Our people say it is a stupid fly that does not know when to quit the stink of a corpse that ends up buried with the corpse as well.

Your majesty, my sister is not stupid. She was raised in a good home and the teachings of my family uphold honesty and integrity. She would never steal from another person. Even if she wanted to steal, she would not be so foolish to risk so much for two yams only, or to steal from this so-called Elder Musa.

But my sister would never steal. My family teaches that we never abandon our family members when they are in need. So, I have been secretly providing for Adamu and my virtuous sister here since Adamu is more concerned with filling his bulging belly with Burukutu than he is with the well-being of my sister."

"It is no secret that Elder Musa wanted my sister as a second wife. Though she is married now, he continues making advances towards her. But she is a virtuous woman and has rebuffed all his advances even though her toad of a husband does not deserve her loyalty. I believe that Elder Musa has perpetrated this insane lie because he is jealous, and his ego is bruised."

Elder Musa shook his head but knew better than to speak until asked to present his accusation. Elder Musa's accusation also hinged on a rebuff of sexual advances, except that he claimed he was the self-respecting adult, not Binta.

Elder Musa's version of events painted a picture of a desperate Binta who had approached him a couple of days before the alleged theft and offered him sexual favors in exchange for some yams.

He refused. He would never touch another man's wife. He had noticed Binta eyeing two yams that he had separated from the rest of his harvest and placed beside his clay pot to be prepared for dinner the next day with palm oil and alligator pepper.

But when it came time for Elder Musa's wife to prepare his dinner, he discovered that the yams had disappeared. Although

Elder Musa accepted that he had no proof, he maintained that there could be no doubt as to whom the culprit was.

Having heard both sides of the story, Habe Nohi paused to reflect. There was silence across the vast inner courtyard. He glanced around the palace again, noticing that Amina and Madaki Zaki had entered the palace through a side door.

Habe Nohi was happy for Amina to observe community matters like this. It was an opportunity for her to gain wisdom. He surveyed his noble council members. They were quiet but thoughtful, ready to provide counsel if called upon. But Habe Nohi would not require their counsel today. He chuckled to himself, enthused by his plan to discover the truth.

Habe Nohi broke the silence, leaning forward as he rubbed the base of his turban. He delivered his verdict.

"Abu. I understand our ancestors have blessed you with a plentiful harvest this year. Therefore, here is my ruling. Give Elder Musa two of your yams as a replacement for the ones he has lost. This does not confer guilt on your sister as there is no proof that she stole his yams.

Rather, I ask as your Habe that you do it as a gesture of peace. I will replace the two yams in your coffers from the royal supply of Zazzau. I will then determine when Binta's husband, Adamu should replenish the royal supply."

"*Madallah!*" Abu and Binta exclaimed and immediately groveled before the Habe, professing their profound gratitude for his wise ruling. But Elder Musa was beside himself with anger.

"Habe Nohi," he began, shaking his head. "Ba haka ba! She is a thief. She must be punished for her dishonest act."

Without prompting, one guard stepped right up to Elder Musa and slapped him hard across his cheek. "Kai, quiet. Speak only when spoken to!"

Elder Musa fell silent and hunched his shoulders. Habe Nohi smiled and settled back onto his throne. He had received the confirmation he had hoped his ruling would expose. Then, he rose, grabbing his golden staff in the process.

The long flowing hem of his babban riga swept the clay floor as he extended his right arm and jammed the bottom end of his staff on the floor to indicate the finality of his decision.

"Elder Musa, our people say water does not sour without a cause. Had you truly been robbed by this young woman, you would have been satisfied with the proposed replenishment of your yams at no cost to you.

Rather, your blind and ill-conceived quest for her punishment has exposed your lies and confirmed her innocence to me. I therefore sentence you to twelve lashes and two weeks of hard labor on the royal farms for wasting my time."

Two guards seized Elder Musa and forced him from the palace amidst great protests and pleas for mercy. Binta and her brother, were cordially escorted from his presence by other guards. Habe Nohi returned to his throne. His noble council members were satisfied and murmured amongst themselves, nodding at the judgment.

Madaki Zaki seized the moment and stepped forward with Amina. He had been standing with Amina close to the palace side door entrance. He greeted his fellow noble council members before bowing to his ruler.

"Ranka ya dade Habe Nohi, your esteemed highness. Our people say water can never be squeezed out of a rock. Wisdom can only exude from he who is worthy. You sir are blessed with the very wisdom of our ancestors. May you live long indeed."

Amina stepped forward from Madaki Zaki's side and rushed to her grandfather.

"*Ranka ya dade* grandfather. May you live long, and may your wisdom grow brighter every day!" she exclaimed as she crossed the short distance to the throne.

Habe Nohi caught her in the billows of his babban riga just as she reached him and flung herself into his embrace. He smiled and held her head close to his chest in warm affection as he looked up at Madaki Zaki.

"Rise, Madaki Zaki," he said. "*Kai ne mai karifi sosai.*"

Madaki Zaki rose and paused for a moment before speaking. Amina, still holding her grandfather tight, caught Madaki Zaki's reprimanding look. She hugged her grandfather a little tighter, looked up at him, and started speaking before Madaki Zaki could. She summarized the events of the evening in a single breath. "Grandfather, please forgive me. I was out on the hills of the Zazzau training valley. I had journeyed to the hills to soak in the beauty of the setting sun from a higher plain and happened to hear distressed cries from a young girl.

This young girl was being attacked by a very vicious man and might have been raped and killed. I could not stand by and allow such a wicked thing to happen. Fortunately, our powerful supreme commander, Madaki Zaki, also heard her cries for help and he rushed to the girl's aid. He overpowered the man and has determined that the wicked man should stand trial before you."

Habe Nohi looked down with some alarm into his granddaughter's eyes and then looked to his warrior commander for explanation.

Madaki Zaki cleared his throat and rolled his eyes. Amina had shaped the narrative in her own mischievous way, omitting parts that could have gotten her in trouble.

"Yes, my esteemed Habe. What your granddaughter has said is in fact true. Although, she left out that she was threatened at knife point by this same wicked man."

"What!" Habe Nohi's eyes now flashed with anger. He could not bear to imagine his precious granddaughter being attacked. "So, not only is this man a rapist but he also threatened to kill my granddaughter? Who is this foolish man, and where is he now?"

The council of noble members remained silent in deference to their ruler, but they also were alarmed by the report that Amina was threatened.

"He is nobody. His name is Mustapha and he is a known criminal. I have ordered my men to return him to the village tonight and throw him in the prison pit until your schedule permits him to be tried and judged."

Habe Nohi relaxed. He cracked a wry smile and looked into Amina's eyes again. "Amina, my little butterfly," he began. "What you did was very brave, and I am proud of you for standing up to the evil man. But you know better than to put yourself in harm's way. What would your mother say if she knew?"

Amina gave a shrug and frowned, looking into Madaki Zaki's eyes. "It is not up to Mama to decide," she retorted. "It is unfair that women are treated differently, that..."

"Be careful, Amina!" Her grandfather's tone was stern. It silenced her. "Be careful Amina," Habe Nohi repeated in a gentler tone. He did not need to say more – his meaning was clear as day.

Amina hugged her grandfather in an unspoken apology. Habe Nohi was aware of Amina's fierce passion for female equality as she had protested inequality to him many times before. He admired her passion though he disagreed with her conviction for equality. He believed a woman should never aspire to be like a man. A woman should be graceful and always show deference to a man.

Habe Nohi gently patted his granddaughter's head. "Alright then, my little butterfly. Go to your mother now. I need to discuss Zazzau affairs with Madaki Zaki and the rest of my noble council."

No sooner had Amina departed the palace than two men in dashikis burst into the palace abruptly, closely followed by three palace guards whose job it was to man the immediate exterior of the palace.

Madaki Zaki, who had just taken a seat among his fellow noble council members, sprang to his feet. "What is the meaning of this sudden disturbance? Have you no respect?"

One of the guards spoke. "Esteemed noble council men, Madaki Zaki, sir. My sincere apologies. Ranka ya dade Habe Nohi. Sir, my apologies to you as well. These warriors are representatives of the sentry unit stationed in our distant horizon. They demanded an immediate audience with you as it is a matter of extreme urgency."

Habe Nohi dismissed the preamble with a quick wave of his hand and leaned forward to hear what the urgent matter was. Madaki Zaki also calmed down. He retook his seat.

One of the sentries spoke up, his chest still heaving as he tried to catch his breath while comporting himself in the presence of the most important men of Zazzau.

"*Randa ya dade...*" he began but was interrupted by an impatient Habe Nohi.

"Out with it. Now!"

"Nupeland has moved to attack us sir. Their warriors, led by the Etsu Tsudi himself are rapidly closing in from the south and are now a mere day's ride away from being upon us."

Loud gasps swept across the palace floor. Madaki Zaki was instantly on his feet again. He began pacing.

Habe Nohi's eyes widened in shock but he retained his composure in an instinctive demonstration of resolve to his observant followers. He leaned back in his throne, absorbing the news.

"How many?" Madaki Zaki asked, pausing mid-pace.

"There are probably a few thousands. They are on horseback and on foot."

Madaki Zaki cursed and punched a fist into his palm. "How could we not have known this many were coming before now? There is no other way in from Nupe other than upstream on the Kaduna river. Surely our sentries would have seen their rowboats, canoes and rafts?"

The sentries exchanged nonplussed looks.

Habe Nohi rose, allowing his babban riga to cascade to the floor as he spoke.

"Well, our riverine sentries failed us and must be punished. But that will have to wait. Now we must prepare for battle. We are Zazzau. We do not fear, we do not cower, and we do not falter. We will defend our sovereignty against this Nupe fool.

Madaki Zaki, summon Mai Sihiri. We need him to beseech our ancestors for victory. As for you, I expect a full battle plan when we reconvene in the morning before daylight breaks. Is that clear?"

"Yes, my esteemed Habe," Madaki Zaki said, bowing. "I have always kept my men trained and ready for sudden attacks like this. I already have a battle plan and the men are savvy in it. I will share my battle plan with you in the morning. I will summon Mai Sihiri as you have commanded."

"Very good," Habe Nohi said to Madaki Zaki. He then declared to the rest of the palace occupants. "Speak nothing of this to anyone. We do not want panic to spread. You heard the confidence of our supreme commander. We shall crush this invader with Zazzau power."

CHAPTER THREE

The Weakness of Princess Bakwa

*Weakness is measured by the degree to which
power is yielded to another*

AMINA APPROACHED HER PARENTS' compound with great caution, like a rumor monger seeking to eavesdrop on whispered village secrets in the quiet of night. The compound was located within the broader palace confines close to the palace itself. All the Habe's family members and closest servants lived in a smattering of huts and a few multi-storied mud dwellings organized into small communities in and around the palace. The shoulder-high mud wall kept prying eyes out.

Amina often wished the walls were lower. Lower walls would allow her easily to see when her father was seated outside his dwelling, drinking Burukutu and eating kola nuts. She hated him and sought to avoid him whenever she could.

Amina reached the front of the wall and huddled close to it, keeping her body shielded so she could spy within the compound without being spotted.

She positioned herself close to the small metal front gate that was shut to prevent her mother's goats and chickens from wandering out of the large compound. She peeked through a small aperture in the metal gate.

She sighted her father seated on his favorite wooden stool in front of the lower floor of his dwelling. He was basked in his lazy stupor. His fat legs were spread out like dead logs of wood under his loin cloth. His naked belly, wide as though he swallowed a goat head whole, spilled over his thighs and covered half his loin cloth.

He raised his Burukutu gourd and crashed it against Boko's, his friend, who was seated on a stool next to him. Wine spilled as the gourds clashed and both men laughed heartily at nothing.

Amina's mother, Princess Bakwa, emerged from a hut next to her father's dwelling on the right side. Princess Bakwa was tall and regal. She was effortlessly royal, even when serving Amina's fat oaf father and his leechy companion. Amina considered just how much she looked like her mother. She was almost as tall as her mother now. Like her mother, she had long legs, a high waist, a long face with high cheekbones, and full lips.

Her mother moved graciously, like any princess trained in royal etiquette would. She would make a wonderful Habe, Amina thought. She could be better than any male Habe could ever be. If only she would reject the shackles of meaningless tradition that only existed to inflate the male ego.

Amina's disgust deepened as her mother emerged with the sole purpose of serving her father. The servants, likely dismissed early by her father, were nowhere to be found.

Princess Bakwa carried a large clay gourd filled with what could only be more Burukutu, Amina imagined. Her father had always demanded that his wife serve him herself and not delegate to any of the household servants. Amina believed he loved the feeling of superiority he derived from having the daughter of the Habe, wait on him. She detested him for this.

Princess Bakwa reached her husband and stooped to refill his gourd. Nikitau paid his wife no attention or acknowledgment as she served him. Rather, he continued his pointless conversing and laughing with Boko.

When Princess Bakwa turned her behind towards her husband to refill Boko's gourd as well, Nikitau reached out and grabbed her behind. Princess Bakwa pushed his hand away and stepped away from the pair who burst out laughing.

Amina's stomach turned in disgust and anger.

"*Ji mana*, when will you give me a male child?" Nikitau yelled at Princess Bakwa who shot him a glare. Without a word, she turned sharply and headed back towards her hut.

Both men burst out laughing again and Amina heard her father yell at her mother's retreating figure.

"I'm coming woman. Lie down and wait for me. *Walahi*, we will see if you can produce a male child this time." Nikitau jammed the Burukutu gourd to his lips and chugged away.

Amina boiled over with rage. She suspected that Nikitau would rather her mother never conceived a male child, so he could continue berating her. He appeared to enjoy it that much. She also suspected that Nikitau was happy she had been born female.

If Princess Bakwa, Habe Nohi's only child, remained without a male heir, she would inherit the title from Habe Nohi. But, being a woman in Zazzau, she would have no power at all.

She would be a mere figurehead for the true power would lie solely with Nikitau, her husband.

Sixteen Rain and Harmattan seasons had passed since Amina was born. It was clear to Amina that her mother was unlikely to ever have another child.

Nikitau smiled, allowing himself a dribble of tan colored Burukutu from his drunken lips to his chin. He dropped the Burukutu gourd down on the dusty floor beside him, belched loudly, and wiped the lingering liquid off his chin with the back of his hand.

Amina swallowed hard, suppressing the wave of disgust that swept through her. She would rather be somewhere else now than be near her mother who had allowed herself to be mocked and abused, or near her father whose appetites had so enslaved him that he failed to comprehend just how evident his uselessness was.

But she had been gone from home far too long. She could not risk her mother discovering that she had visited the warrior training ground. Amina opened the gate and began walking toward her mother's hut.

"Amina," her father called out in a loud, brash voice.

Amina cursed under her breath.

"Yes Baba?" she muttered, slowing her walk. She looked up at him. "Tell your mother to bring us some more kola nuts and fresh alligator pepper. And she better hurry. If I must wait for a male child, I do not need to wait for everything else."

Amina gritted her teeth and clenched a fist. She took a couple of deep breaths to calm the rage that welled up inside her.

"Yes Baba," she replied as calmly as she could and proceeded to her mother's hut with her face down and her eyes stinging from holding back angry tears.

Princess Bakwa heard her husband's hurtful words. She had set about her task, retrieving choice kola nuts from a large calabash in a corner of the hut, and placing them into a small wooden bowl.

Amina stared at her mother. Why would she allow herself to be disrespected time and time again? Why should men always have the upper hand?

Amina finally summoned the courage to table a request she had been meaning to make for a very long time. She walked up behind her mother and opened her mouth. But the brimming rage within her betrayed words that went far beyond the controversial request she had intended to make.

"Mama, I hate that Baba speaks to you this way and you allow it. Why would you allow it? Why?

I hate that we accept and uphold a culture where men have total authority over women and are considered better than women in everything. Give me your blessing so I can ask Madaki Zaki to teach me the way of the Sojojin Zazzau, and I swear to you, I will protect you from Baba or any other man who dares disrespect you. I will be a better warrior than any man has ever been."

Princess Bakwa stiffened, remaining motionless for what seemed an eternity.

The silence that ensued was palpable. Amina felt fear crash against her resolve like angry waves thrashing a beach. It was unheard of for a woman to even consider performing a man's duty. And here she was, not only asking for permission to participate in what was considered the manliest duty of all, but also scolding her mother while doing so.

Finally, Princess Bakwa rose. She turned to face her daughter, her eyes flashing with anger like fiery balls of fire. When she spoke, her voice was low yet louder in force than the angriest storm.

"Hear me, child. Let this be the first and the last time I ever hear you utter such words to me or to anyone at all. You are lucky that I have enough restraint to keep this hands that cradled you as a baby from raining slaps upon you.

But do not test me again, child. I assure you that next time, I shall not be so merciful. And hear me, you must never ever challenge Baba's actions. You are getting too bold for your own good. Now take this bowl of kola nuts to Baba and his friend."

As Amina exited the hut with the bowl of kola nuts in hand, Princess Bakwa sank to her knees. She allowed tears she had held back to overwhelm her.

"Why Mama, why did you consent to me marrying this horrible man?"

Her deceased mother, Queen Shettima, taught her from a very early age, that a woman should never oppose her husband.

"Why am I cursed with such a terrible husband when you were blessed with our Habe, a man who treated you with grace and respect? Here I am, bound body and soul in a marriage I am forbidden to complain about. Mama, you are with our ancestors now. I beseech you to look upon your daughter with mercy and somehow deliver me from this prison."

CHAPTER FOUR

More than a Friend

There is no truer test of friendship than desire sacrificed for the one who is called friend

JAMILA, AMINA'S PUDGY-FACED best friend was seated outside her mother's mud hut a stone's throw southeast of the palace in the southern dwelling corridor of Zazzau. She had two metal basins before her. One was filled with freshly harvested corn, the other contained a few cobs of peeled corn.

On the dusty ground next to the basins, a pile of peeled husks was building. Jamila was hard at work, peeling off corn husks and preparing the corn for threshing and grinding.

Jamila looked up just as her friend, Amina walked through her compound's open gates. Her countenance brightened, and she rose to curtsy as a customary show of respect for royalty.

"*Sannu da Zuwa*," Jamila offered, smiling.

Amina smiled in return before frowning at her friend's formal gesture. She was glad to have Jamila as a friend and as an outlet for the frustration.

"Oh stop," Amina started. She saw Jamila's mother, Fatima, appear in the doorway of the hut. She immediately understood why Jamila had upheld protocol.

Their tight bond of friendship had long superseded the requirement for formal displays of respect. But protocol and custom had to be upheld where others were present.

Fatima curtsied to her, inquired after her parent's health, and as to whether her visit was for royal business or pleasure.

Amina affirmed that her parents were in good health and thanked Fatima for her kind words. She clarified that her visit was for pleasure. Fatima smiled and told Amina that she was always welcome. She then glanced at her daughter and the two metal basins before her.

"Jamila," she began, her tone infused with both exasperation and disappointment at the same time. "The sun is setting, and you have barely made any progress with the corn. What have you been doing?"

Amina spoke before her friend could make an excuse.

"Mama Jamila," she said. "I will help Jamila so we can make progress together."

Fatima looked alarmed. "Haba, bana soun wannan fa! You are Princess Bakwa's daughter. I don't want trouble."

Amina smiled. "Mama Jamila, please. Jamila is my friend. Let me help. Many hands make lighter duty. It is no trouble, I promise."

Fatima considered for a while, then looking at the fast setting sun. "Alright, Princess Amina. But please only for a brief while. The sun is going to sleep, and you must return home soon before your parents miss you."

Amina set to work helping her friend and Fatima, satisfied with the compromise, left the girls to their task.

When Fatima was out of earshot, Amina shared what she had just witnessed at her parents.

Jamila listened as Amina summarized the events.

"Amina, I completely see why you would be so upset. The way your father treats your mother is despicable. And to make matters worse, she is the Habe's daughter. It is only because he is a man that he can get away with such disrespect to your mother.

It is not the first time you have shared a story like this with me, so you probably know what my response is likely to be. I will always take your side my dear. But, Amina, I must warn you to be careful. We are still young girls, and even if we were grown, we are women and..."

Amina slammed a corn cob she had just unsheathed into one of the metal basins.

"No!" she exclaimed. "*Ba baka ba*! Young girls, full grown women, it does not matter. It does not mean that we should remain silent while being taken advantage of."

"Amina, calm down. I agree with you. I am not the enemy. Our elders say wisdom to the foolish is like water clasped in a fist but to the wise, it is like refreshing water stored in an earthen vessel. Angry outbursts or actions will never turn things around. If you really want to change things, you must be patient and wise like the old tortoise who somehow manages to outlive the fastest and fiercest animals in the forest."

Amina stared wide-eyed at her friend like she had done so many times in the past when Jamila displayed wisdom well beyond her years. Jamila was slightly younger than she was and was shorter and stouter. What she lacked in regal stature, Jamila compensated for in wisdom. Amina laughed.

"Ok, my wise friend, you are right again. That is why I come to you when I am upset."

Jamila brushed off the awkwardness with laughter and patted her friend on the back. She hugged her.

"Don't worry. I know you will find your way through this. You are much wiser than you give yourself credit for. And...you give me too much credit by the way. It is easy for me to be calm because although my mother was one of three wives when my father was still alive, he treated them equally and fairly. Now that he has passed on, she is her own master."

She paused, then added.

"Although, that won't last much longer if Mahmud's father, Mallam Sule, continues to visit her as often as he does."

Amina's eyes widened in surprise and she slapped her friend on the back. "*Fada gaskiya aboki na?* Is your mother really being courted? Isn't she too old for that?"

Jamila laughed out loud. "Well, apparently not, considering the twinkle in his eyes whenever he visits. He usually brings his son

Mahmud with him under the pretense of lending a helping hand to my single mother.

But I know why he really comes here. I don't mind so long as he doesn't make her his third wife. It has been almost ten seasons since my father passed on and since she is a grown woman, she does not need anyone's permission for a man to take care of her."

Amina laughed again. "It seems to me that he might need your permission to proceed."

Both girls were quiet for a while, each buried in thought and focused on the task at hand.

Amina was thinking how it might be a good thing if her mother was to divorce her husband and be courted by someone else. But she knew that the Zazzau custom forbade such a thing. Once a woman married, death was the only thing that could separate her from her husband.

Distracted by her worrisome thoughts, Amina did not see the husk hurled at her until it hit her head. Jamila erupted in laughter as Amina shrieked.

"Got you!" Jamila said, reaching for the pile of husks in anticipation of her friend's retaliation.

Amina was on her feet quickly. She wasted no time in firing off a few husks at her friend but not before she had been on the receiving end of a few more herself. Both girls squealed with laughter as the corn husks flew in either direction and each tried to dodge the onslaught from the other.

After a while, Amina held up her hand. "Ok stop. There's only one way to settle this. We settle it like we always do – competition."

Jamila paused, poised for a throw. Her laughing eyes beamed.

"And what exactly do you have in mind, dear princess?"

"The one who can throw the corn husk the farthest is the winner," Amina said, as though the game she had just proposed was a standard sport – the rules of which were indisputable.

"Winner of what?" Jamila asked.

Amina hadn't quite thought that through. She paused and rolled her eyes.

"Let me help you there," Jamila said.

"Everyone knows there are only so many handsome young men in the village that are truly worthy of you or me. So, I say the winner gets to pick the choicest boyfriend first."

Amina burst out laughing and declared. "I like that! Why shouldn't women be allowed to pick whom they court, just like the men do? Let them see how it is to be selected like a choice piece of antelope meat, no?"

Jamila caught the infectious mirth and soon, both girls were laughing out loud.

Their playful digression attracted supervision. A stern voice brought them back to reality.

"Jamila! What is all this nonsense? You have littered the whole place with corn husks and are still yet to complete what I have asked of you."

Fatima once again stood in the open doorway of her hut, arms folded across her chest. A deep frown creased into her forehead.

Both Jamila and Amina scurried back to their work positions. "I am sorry Mama," Jamila said with feigned contrition. "We will work hard now and clean up when we are finished."

Fatima glared at the backs of both girls for a moment, as though she might sear their backs with the burn of disapproval from her eyes.

"You better hurry. No more playing or I will have you spend your entire day tomorrow doing nothing but this as well."

With that, Fatima disappeared once more into her hut, leaving the mischievous, giggling girls to focus on their assigned duty.

As they poured themselves into the task at hand, Amina found herself thinking about how much she valued Jamila's friendship. They had become friends when they were both barely five years old.

Jamila had lost her father, Babayaro, to a strange illness. One day he was a big strong man, healthy and dependable. The next day he was a shadow of himself, bed-ridden and barely able to talk. He had depreciated rather quickly, losing a chunk of his body and soul each day until he finally expired.

Jamila and her mother had been inconsolable at the funeral which was attended by most in Zazzau for Babayaro was well known and beloved by the community. At the funeral, little Amina, listening to Jamila's heart wrenching wailing, felt moved with compassion.

Amina had walked up to Jamila and given her a shoulder to cry on. It was a sight that brought fresh tears to the eyes of all observing villagers. For Jamila and Amina, it was the beginning of a special friendship that had grown and strengthened since that funeral day.

As they worked in silence some more, Amina reached out and put her left arm around her friend's shoulder.

"Thank you for being my friend," she said, smiling.

Jamila looked her friend in the eye and nodded in acknowledgment. "Your transparent attempt to soften me up won't buy you the rights to the choicest young man in the village. That is a competition that still needs to happen."

Amina laughed and slapped her friend on the back again.

"*Sannu Ku, yaya gida?*" a deep male voice said. Both girls looked up. Standing beside the open metal gate at the compound entrance was a tall thin man. Beside him, there was an equally tall but much more muscular younger man.

"Ah, Baba Mahmud, *lafiya lau*," Jamila replied. "It is good to see you sir." Jamila's eyes shifted to the young man standing next to Baba Mahmud and she inadvertently batted her eyes. "Mahmud, it is good to see you again as well."

Mahmud nodded in acknowledgment, but his eyes were fixed on Amina.

Jamila quickly introduced the visitors to the princess so that they would pay their respects. Amina smiled at the guests' surprised looks. She knew most villagers would not recognize her as she typically hid her face behind a veil during public functions or when visiting the village. Both Mahmud and his father paid Amina homage, bowing.

Jamila frowned at Mahmud. "Mahmud. Stop staring, you will make Princess Amina nervous."

Mahmud averted his eyes. "I was not staring," he said before glancing at his father for a reaction. Baba Mahmud did not react to his son. Instead, he addressed Jamila, his voice betraying some impatience.

"Is your mother home?"

Amina found herself enjoying Mahmud's embarrassment. She had never received attention from a boy before. Was he staring at her because he was in awe of her royalty? She found that she enjoyed the attention.

"Yes, yes, she is," Jamila replied to Baba Mahmud, her eyes barely leaving Mahmud who had resumed staring at Amina.

Amina examined Mahmud as well. He was a handsome boy, growing a mustache and a beard with sideburns that complemented his square jaw.

Baba Mahmud walked past the girls, leaving his son with instructions to assist the girls with the task at hand. Mahmud seemed to recover from his trance upon hearing his father's instruction.

"Mahmud, you are welcome to join us like your father instructed," Jamila called out, flashing him the sweetest smile.

Amina heard the lure in her friend's voice and observed her demeanor as she called to him. Jamila obviously liked this boy, but he seemed unconcerned by her. Amina liked that she had captured his attention. It made her feel powerful.

CHAPTER FIVE

Tsudi – Etsu of Nupe

Ambition is a two-faced monster that lives deep within every man's soul

Seven Days Earlier

THIN STREAMS OF EMERGING sunlight shone through several crevices on the wooden side of a large, bronze rowboat slowly edging towards a grassy shoreline.

The sun rays lined the face of a middle-aged man who was asleep on a straw mat inside the rowboat. The man's eyelids fluttered, disturbed by the offending light. He tried to open his eyes but was blinded by the sunlight. He shut his eyes again and yawned, stretching long and wide. He must have slept for a long time.

He sat up and rubbed his eyes, allowing a moment to recollect his surroundings. The enclosed wooden interior of the rowboat was small, and mostly bare except for the mat he slept on, an oil lamp, and some food which consisted of mostly dried bread and yams.

All that remained were the weapons and royal gifts his father had provided for his journey and safety. He surveyed the wooden bows and arrows with metal points, the royal brass bangles, the iron ankle chains believed to be infused with protective magic.

Then, he let his eyes fall on the most precious of all the gifts – the bronze finger ring that had belonged to his father. The ring, the bangles, and the magic chains were the only evidence of the royalty that he was and the royalty he was meant to be – Tsudi, Ata of the Igala village.

Tsudi gritted his teeth in anger and chewed, from habit, on his disfigured lip. His lip was disfigured from a fall he suffered several seasons ago in Idah, the capital of the Igala village, where he had lived for the past fifteen seasons.

He had climbed a tall tree, braving a violent thunderstorm and the tree's forbidding height to pluck its sacred fruit. This sacred fruit was prophesied, by the village sorcerer, to be the only thing that could heal his father, the Ata, who was gravely ill at the time.

It was an impossible fall to survive. But Tsudi did survive it. And he managed to pluck the fruit.

Tsudi's courageous act had further endeared him to his father, greatly enhancing his chance of becoming the next Ata much to the chagrin of his two half-brothers – Maazu and Jibiri.

Tsudi's half-brothers' displeasure evolved into such terrible hate and envy that his father sent him away before he fell victim to the scheming duo.

Tsudi fled Idah enroute to Nupeko – one of Igala's riverine vassal villages. Nupeko was where Tsudi originated from. Now, many seasons after, he was heading back home to assume kingship of the vassal village.

Tsudi rose. The rowboat was small, and he could rise only to a limited degree. He started towards a small ragged curtain leading to the open deck of the rowboat. There, his trusted advisor, Mokwa, was commanding twelve Igala strongmen fully occupied with rowing the boat to Nupeko.

Mokwa was a tall man who towered a full head above Tsudi. Tsudi's father had searched long and hard in Igala for an advisor to his son. In Mokwa, he found an enviable combination of physical strength and wisdom.

Mokwa had been leading the strongmen for days now, urging them to row to Nupeko as quickly as they could. Tsudi realized they were nearing the shores of Nupeko now and his thoughts centered on the village of his birth as he approached the deck entrance.

His mother in Nupeko had died of a stomach sickness when he was just a little boy. Rather than have him become a burden, the village elders had decided that he be sent to Idah as a slave tribute. It had been custom for five strong and healthy boys to be delivered to Idah as slave tribute to assist on the farms each season just before the rains began.

Tsudi had, for a long time, resented his village. But his resentment was long gone. Though the village had abandoned him to enslavement, that action had connected him with his father.

Long ago, the Ata of Idah had visited Nupeko as was customary. As a gesture of goodwill, the vassal king of Nupeko had offered the Ata one of the most beautiful maidens in the village.

The Ata had been smitten by the beauty of the maiden and enjoyed a night of pleasure with her. Unknown to him, a child, Tsudi, was conceived that night.

The Ata had left a seal of approval with the maiden that night – a royal bronze ring. Years later, he had discovered the ring on the boy slave Tsudi. The boy slave told the Ata that the ring had been given to his deceased mother by his father, a father he didn't know.

The vassal king of Nupeko had recently died of old age and now that the forty-day mandatory mourning period was complete, Tsudi's father was seizing the opportunity to install his beloved son as king of his mother's people in Nupeko.

Tsudi was eager to fulfill his royal destiny. He had dreams of establishing a vibrant Nupe community along the boundary creeks of the great River Niger and its main tributary - River Kaduna.

He had visions of one day expanding the Nupe community into an empire as far north as possible towards the Hausa villages. He aspired to someday return southwards after his father had passed to wrest control of Igala from whichever half-brother would be king in future. He was, after all, the favorite heir of the Ata of Igala.

Tsudi emerged onto the open deck of the rowboat. His nostrils were greeted with the freshness of morning dew. His ears perked up to the chirping of birds nestled in the chaos of trees on the beckoning grassy banks of Nupeko some distance ahead.

Tsudi sighed and yawned again, making a loud noise that caught the attention of his traveling companions. The bare-chested Igala strongmen were seated in columns of six on either side of the rowboat, paddling in rhythm to a famous Igala folk song.

Mokwa heard Tsudi emerge and turned to greet him. He observed the young, fearless warrior he was sworn to protect. Tsudi was taller than most men with fierce features that could only have been given by the ancestors to one who was born to war. His face was long and thin with his facial skin stretched as though there was barely enough to cover the length of his skull. His eyes were stern and bulbous like two large oranges protruding from his thin face.

"My lord Tsudi. I trust you are well-rested," Mokwa said.

Tsudi nodded and waved him back to his task of motivating the rowers.

"Who are we?" Mokwa called out in a deep baritone.

"Igala's power," the rowing crew replied in unison.

"Why are we?"

"Because we conquer."

Tsudi noticed a change in the rowing pattern of the strongmen. It suddenly became urgent, frantic even. He began turning to Mokwa for an explanation. But there was no need. Mokwa was by his side in a flash, his face now a cloud of concern. Mokwa's eyes were like a cat's – large and round with thin slit pupils. Now his eyes widened even more.

"My lord Tsudi," Mokwa began with a low, respectful bow, "You must exit the boat now and swim to the grassy banks of Nupeko. Take the bronze ring your father gave you as proof of your lineage and heritage. There must be no doubt that the Ata himself sent you even though you arrive on Nupeko's shores with neither slave nor warrior to herald your arrival. You must leave at once. Hurry..."

There was no movement.

"Please, go now!" Mokwa's voice flooded with alarm and he began pushing Tsudi.

"What is this disrespect?" Tsudi asked.

"I am sorry my lord," Mokwa offered, shrinking backwards and forcing his hands down to his sides. Tsudi's anger faded as he could see Mokwa's alarm. What could be so troubling?

"What is it Mokwa, tell me?" Tsudi's voice took on an urgent tone. "What is it?"

Mokwa kept his gaze locked on Tsudi.

"My lord, it is your brothers. They are in pursuit and not far behind. I had thought we could outrun them, but they have been gaining on us for a while.

Your father kept his plans for you a secret from them. I fear that if we dock at Nupeko, your father's plans will be laid bare. I am certain that your brothers have warriors with them and will stop at nothing to kill you and whomever stands in their way at Nupeko.

Therefore, I am afraid we must create a diversion. You need to exit the rowboat quietly but swiftly. We will lead them astray by continuing upstream on River Kaduna or perhaps we shall head west on the Niger."

Tsudi gulped. His departure had been secretly planned and executed. How could his brothers have found out and so soon too? But there was no time to ponder.

"But they will catch up with you soon no matter what path you take. Then what?"

Even as Tsudi asked the question, he knew the answer. The strongmen had sworn to protect him with their lives. They were prepared to make good on their oaths.

It was futile trying to imagine alternatives. Mokwa had made it clear there was no time for that and that he was determined to protect his master, even if it meant pushing him overboard to save his life.

Tsudi demanded to see his would-be attackers for himself, grabbing the makeshift bamboo telescope from Mokwa in exasperation. Whether armed with a thousand fiercely armed warriors or with nothing but their fists alone, his two half-brothers did not scare him.

Tsudi took courage in the fact that he had cheated death quite a few times. Whenever death was finally ready to collect its due, it would surely send him notice beforehand – a show of respect for the games they had played, all of which he had won thus far.

Squinting to see as far as he could through the bamboo telescope, Tsudi noticed three black dots on the horizon against the backdrop of the rising sun.

By estimation, they were probably less than half a day's journey behind. These rowboats could carry up to seventy-five men. Mokwa was right. Tsudi realized it was wise to escape while he could.

He handed the bamboo telescope back to Mokwa, his face stern in deep contemplation. He brimmed with anger at being exiled this way. He swore to one day return to Igala and claim the throne which was rightfully his.

River Kaduna felt anything but wet as Tsudi lowered himself into it, careful to avoid a splash. Strangely, his feet felt wet, but the rest of his body didn't. He reached down to his feet, to touch the river. But he awoke to the feeling of rain splatter on his legs, blowing into his mud hut from a rainstorm outside.

Tsudi sat up suddenly on his raffia mat and waited for his eyes to adjust to the darkness. He glanced across from him. Lempe, his second of four wives lay sprawled naked beside him on another raffia mat.

He had fallen asleep after a night of pleasure and did not realize that Lempe had failed to return to her mud hut next to his. He hissed with disdain and considered waking her to send her to her hut. But his mind had no room for things of little consequence now. His dream had been quite vivid. But it was no simple dream – it was a recollection of the events that had led to his return to Nupeko about fifteen seasons ago.

Tsudi rose and trudged into an inner chamber carved out of his hut.

He emerged moments later, clad in a thin black cloth tightly wrapped around his torso and knotted on his right shoulder. He grabbed a small straw mat to protect himself from the rain and headed out to his palace courtyard, braving the rainstorm outside enroute Mokwa's hut.

"We need to wait just a little while longer, my lord Tsudi," Mokwa said. He was seated on a straw mat on the floor next to his king, Etsu Tsudi, whom he had presented with a wooden chair and footstool for added comfort.

The two were alone in Mokwa's main hut, the largest of three huts in his courtyard. The other two huts belonged to his two wives and children.

Mokwa had been alarmed waking up to the silhouette of Etsu Tsudi standing in his doorway with a powerful rainstorm thrashing behind him amidst flashes of lightning and the cracking of thunder.

Etsu Tsudi's guards had come rushing in moments later, desperate to explain that they had tried, to no avail, to persuade the Etsu to return to his palace until the morning when it would be safe and dry. But Etsu Tsudi refused to heed the guards' counsel for he was greatly troubled.

"Every day we wait, Zazzau strengthens and Igala slips further from my grip. We have gained control of two Nupe villages along the Niger. That gives us greater strength in numbers. We must strike now!"

Etsu Tsudi spoke with exasperation, and his eyes seemed to glow with anger against the dim lighting provided by an oil lamp attached to a metal wire hanging low from the roof of Mokwa's hut.

Mokwa looked down, pausing for a moment. Then he spoke.

"My lord Tsudi. I understand the urgency to attack Zazzau. I realize that victory against Zazzau will provide us with the nearest geographical access to Hausaland. This access will open a channel to the Arabian trade routes up north leading to Cairo and Alexandria. I know that victory will also equip us with slaves and spoil useful for your ultimate plan to attack Igala and claim your rightful place as Ata.

My lord, although I deeply comprehend these valid reasons to strike Zazzau imminently, I must uphold my paramount duty to provide you with counsel. My counsel to you is that we must be assured of victory before we strike.

Our people say if a child is found walking alone in the night, then there must be an elder somewhere behind him for protection. If we attack now, we will be like a child who ventures into the night with no elder behind him."

Mokwa paused and then looked up at his king.

"Have I not always given you sound counsel, my lord Tsudi? Did I not risk my life and that of twelve others to protect you when we first came to this land fifteen seasons ago?

Had we not led your half-brothers upstream on River Kaduna and then eluded them by secretly abandoning the rowboat, we would surely have perished at their hands for your sake. Then we undertook the dangerous task of swimming down River Kaduna for several days to rejoin you in Nupeko."

Mokwa paused again, then continued.

"We almost died. But we accomplished the impossible because our ancestors were with us. We survived because our ancestors are watching over you. They wanted us to return to you to serve as the wind beneath your wings.

It is my solemn belief that our ancestors want you to rule Nupe and to expand this land like never before. You will rule from the far northern heights of Hausaland in the ancient city of Kano to the southern border of Igala beyond the great River Niger. But I must beg you to be patient, so we do not subvert destiny."

Mokwa paused for yet another moment before making his next point. Seeing he still had his leader's consideration, he continued.

"It is true that we have control of Kusapa and Batachi, two of Nupe's clans. But, my lord, there are eight more clans of the confederacy that we are yet to control. The remaining eight still pay tribute to Igala and will not ally with us or submit to you.

Therefore, I believe we must intensify our work on the shores of the Niger to frustrate these clans economically. Their farmers and fishermen must be taxed more for their produce so that they will be forced to pressure their leaders into submitting to your leadership.

My lord, even if we only wait until we have support from five of the ten, that will put us in a much stronger position to invade Zazzau. However, to forge a true and powerful alliance, we must coerce them to yield of their own accord. They must not be conquered through war as they are your mother's people. Violence against one's own people is akin to slitting one's wrist.

My humble advice, my lord, is that we should wait until we have a broad alliance with the Nupe confederacy to attack Zazzau. If we do this right, our attack on Zazzau will be the spark that starts the campaign we desire; a campaign that will conclude in victory over all Hausaland and ultimately, Igala."

Etsu Tsudi waited for Mokwa to finish speaking. He had suspected his trusted advisor would not support his decision to attack Zazzau now. Mokwa was always so cautious. He hated to admit it but Mokwa's counsel had always served him well.

Nonetheless, Etsu Tsudi was restless. He had recently received news that his father had passed away and, to his chagrin, that his half-brother Maazu had assumed leadership of Igala as the new Ata.

This unsettling news had fueled Etsu Tsudi's impatience. He was desperate to strike fear into his half-brother's heart, and to send him an unmistakable signal that Etsu Tsudi, the rightful Ata, was on a war path.

What better way to signal this than to invade Hausaland? News of his Zazzau conquest would carry far and wide and would surely rattle Maazu.

"Mokwa, thank you for your counsel. But I have decided. We must attack now. Ready our warriors with a battle plan and summon Majiya so we might consult our ancestors and understand what must be done to guarantee victory. We shall attack Zazzau in seven days from today."

CHAPTER SIX

Nupe vs. Zazzau

In battle, there are neither winners nor losers.
There are only dead men departed too soon

AMID DUST SWIRLING IN intermittent gusts of wind on a great wide plain, a white battle-ready horse stood lined with magical black cowries and mounted with a saddle made from black mamba skin.

This horse stood before a formidable army of warriors, spread far and wide like sands of the Sahara Desert. These warriors, the Sojojin Zazzau, were poised and battle-ready.

Madaki Zaki sat still atop the white horse, in front of the formidable sands of the Sahara. His shining bald head reflected, like a mirror, the blazing sun high in the Zazzau sky.

Madaki Zaki's face was a mask of menace, a scowl etched permanently in his features like a sea lion's whiskers. His eyes were thin behind dark rings painted in charcoal. His right hand clutched a long, metal spear.

The sharp end of his spear pointed towards the sunny sky and shone bright enough to blind the gluttonous eyes of blackbirds already circling the battle field.

Madaki Zaki spat on the earth beside him and wiped drool off his lips with the back of his palm. No man, whether slave dog or royal prince, would successfully challenge Zazzau's Habe so long as he was alive.

Perhaps Madaki Zaki's stone-faced calm in the face of several thousand battle-crazed Nupe warriors charging towards him should have served as a warning to the empire-seeking aggressors.

Perhaps the ominous serenity of the mighty warriors behind Madaki Zaki, skins coated in charcoal and shaven heads salved with the Zazzau traditional ointment of invincibility, should have served as warning to the onrushing Nupe foot soldiers and galloping cavalry.

But it seemed to Madaki Zaki that the Nupe aggressors had shredded all fabric of caution, perhaps intoxicated by grandiose promises of reward by their leader.

Madaki Zaki could see Etsu Tsudi in the distance, poised high on a black horse. He observed Etsu Tsudi motionless and observant at the spot where the charge had begun.

Etsu Tsudi looked like a commander supremely confident that his warriors would battle to the death for him. He was adorned in a long hyena-skin cloak and covered in amulets and brass chains which probably harbored ancestral magical powers.

A moment ago, Madaki Zaki had seen him propel his Nupe warriors into attack with a war-cry akin to a jackal's howl. Now the Etsu's warriors charged, machetes brandished, and spears held high.

The promise of victory was perhaps no less real to them than the Harmattan-scented air they inhaled with each passing moment. Etsu Tsudi's war-cry rang loud across the battle horizon, and adrenalin coursed through the veins of his charging warriors.

Madaki Zaki had heard rumors that Etsu Tsudi gained Nupe alliances by economic means but also through trepidation. When he conquered some paltry surrounding settlements outside Nupe and forcibly annexed them to the Nupe confederacy, he ensured that news of his brutal methods spread across the entire Nupe land.

He collected bloodied, decapitated heads on stakes and paraded them as victory trophies on the outskirts of his palace for days -- a morbid warning to any who would oppose him or doubt his ruthlessness.

The charging Nupe warriors closed in rapidly on the stoic Sojojin Zazzau. Waist down, the Nupe warriors were skirted in sunbaked antelope skin. Their bare feet, arms, and cheeks were smeared in mud.

The charging Nupe warriors surged still. The men raged, their chests heaving, and sweat pouring down their glistening skins like torrents of the great River Niger after a massive rainfall.

The horses galloped, foaming at the mouth with jaws clamped on rope bits at bridle ends. As the warriors closed in on the Sojojin Zazzau, the galloping cavalry drew even closer.

Running Nupe bowmen, hundreds of them, now stopped on cue. They had reached shooting distance and were readying to draw first blood. They began spreading out, ready to unleash poisoned arrows on their stoic foes.

At that moment, Madaki Zaki raised his spear high into the sky and, with a swift motion brought its rear end crashing down, splitting earth and raising dust. The earth around him reverberated from the force of the smashing thud. It was an unmistakable signal.

They suddenly sprang to life. Fierce Zazzau fighters on foot and horseback, armed with clubs, machetes, swords and spears, erupted on either side of the surrounding hills like termites pouring down an anthill into the valley plain.

Zazzau bowmen appeared like phantom creatures, rapidly forming a towering wall of attack faster than the startled Nupe aggressors could comprehend.

Suddenly, Nupe notions of victory expired faster than the morning dew in the wake of the rising sun. Zazzau bowmen, covered in bronze ornaments and magic chains, formed a wall on either edge of the valley and crouched. They drew arrows from leather quivers loosely hung on their backs, stretched their bows and fired arrows in rapid succession.

The arrows soared high into the sky and far across the plain before arching downwards with tips aflame, raining down like a hurricane of fire onto the Nupe warriors in the battle valley.

All too soon, the Nupe were outnumbered and outwitted, trapped and terrified like deer in a lion's den.

Madaki Zaki seized the moment and thundered his battle cry.

As his warriors exploded past him onto the battle field with gleaming machetes and spears raised towards their terror-stricken opponents, Madaki Zaki swung off his horse, landing on his toes. He tossed his spear a few inches high and caught it horizontally, gripping it at the middle. He aimed, broke into a small run and unleashed a powerful throw.

Madaki Zaki's target, Etsu Tsudi, looked just as taken aback by the sudden turn of events on the battle field as his panicked charges were. As Etsu Tsudi lifted his gaze from the valley towards Madaki Zaki, his eyes flooded with a crazed mix of panic and desperation.

Madaki Zaki's spear was on course for his heart. Etsu Tsudi dodged, moving as quickly as he could. The spear missed his heart and struck his left shoulder, ripping flesh and drawing a massive burst of blood as it lifted him like a rag doll from his horse and threw him to the ground.

Etsu Tsudi howled in agony, clutching his punctured shoulder as the spear clattered to the dusty earth, its tip covered with his flesh and blood.

The valley was now ablaze with fire and fury. Zazzau warriors had descended on the Nupe warriors and a butcher's carnage was being smeared on the dusty earth's canvas. There was writhing and crying in agony as machetes sliced into their targets and blood sprouted like sap from felled trees.

Madaki Zaki had joined the slaughter. Wielding an axe in one hand and a machete in the other, he charged onto the valley of death now strewn with severed limbs, carcasses ablaze, and wounded men pleading for death's mercy.

As Madaki Zaki moved deftly, he raised his axe and landed it on a mud-smeared skull rushing to attack him. It collapsed like a coconut and blood trickled first. Then, it erupted in a fountain as Madaki Zaki forcibly withdrew his axe.

Madaki Zaki moved deeper into the battle field, stabbing or severing any fiends that moved in his pathway. He was powerful, fearless and, merciless. He executed judgment swiftly.

The Sojojin Zazzau were merciless in their butchery of the Nupe aggressors. Mud-smeared fighting men and their horses fell like bothersome fruit flies swatted on a hot sweaty day. All who attempted to flee were seized and set ablaze.

Mokwa and a few others on horseback, had stayed behind with the Etsu while the Nupe warriors charged forward. These aides now aided their stricken leader to his feet.

Etsu Tsudi, clutching his battered shoulder while cursing Zazzau a thousand times over, rose with significant effort. The Nupe warriors had been outnumbered. Etsu Tsudi was helped onto one of his aide's horses and rushed from the battle area in a dusty cloud of undignified haste.

◆◆◆

The Aftermath of Battle in Zazzau: One day Later

"Aiyeeeeeeee," a jubilant fever pitched cry rang out before thousands of joyous Zazzau village folk clustered in a rectangular formation around the perimeter of the Zazzau village square.
The cry was followed by an extended blare from a polished elephant tusk. These were the imperious proclamations of victory that emanated from Ali, Zazzau's vivacious royal storyteller who was leading a trio of uniformed warriors on ornamented horseback into the village square.

Madaki Zaki sat in the middle of the trio observing the celebration and beaming with pride.

The uniformed riders were closely followed by a troupe of male dancers and drummers who, prompted by Ali's victorious trumpeting, began a marvelous sequence of acrobatic dance celebrations in rhythm to a symphony of pulsating drumbeats. Members of the dance troupe were dressed in elegant traditional attire to celebrate the momentous occasion.

The dancers wore bright blue and yellow wrappers that appeared to dazzle as they danced. Their ankles, waists, and necks were decorated with plentiful beads and their heads were beautified with elaborate headgear plumed with peacock feathers. Their faces were painted in red and white – white for peace and red for the blood that had been spilled to purchase peace.

Ali darted into the village square, convulsing like a possessed man and recounting as loudly as he could, the highlights of Zazzau's victory over the invading Nupe scoundrels. His rendition layered in rich detail and imagination, even espousing the motives of the strongmen that led their warriors into battle.

Ali described how embarrassed and humiliated Tsudi must have felt. He questioned how the Nupe, a people inspired by Tsudi, once a common slave, could ever dare to invade Zazzau.

"How could a common slave, a dog, dare to challenge the honorable Habe of Zazzau, Habe Nohi?" he asked the crowd. They were enthralled by his oration and cheered him on.

The riders came to a stop in the middle of the village square and the accompanying dance troupe fanned out in a semi-circle around the horsemen. They continued dancing with Ali, drawing gasps, laughter and applause at the dexterity of their synchronized dance and acrobatic moves.

At the far south end of the village square, close to the entrance leading to the palace courtyard, the royal family was seated, observing the celebratory proceedings with great pride and satisfaction.

Habe Nohi was seated on a makeshift wooden throne. He wore a white babban riga and a regal purple turban befitting of the occasion. On one side, Amina and her mother, Princess Bakwa, sat on tall wooden stools, adorned in embroidered purple wrappers. On his other side, Nikitau, dressed like his father-in-law, was seated on a tall wooden stool as well.

Behind the royal family, their plethora of royal servants stood in perfect rows and columns also observing the proceedings with glee.

After a few more moments of euphoric dancing, Madaki Zaki held his hand up high, bringing the celebrations to a temporary halt.

He motioned instructions to his uniformed companions who had ridden with him into the square and they immediately complied. The companions, Ahmed, his assistant, and Bello, an exemplary warrior, drew bows from the leather quivers strapped on their backs and with little pause fired off successive arrows in the direction of the village square entrance.

Their arrows struck their intended targets with enough speed and precision to kill. The targets were the bloodied corpses of Nupe warriors hanging on wooden stakes. The warriors' archery was merely a small reenactment of Zazzau's triumph, a part of the customary celebrations. As the arrows tore into the corpses like sandbags, a roar of approval and sustained applause erupted from the onlooking crowd.

Madaki Zaki, still atop his horse turned his animal around to face Habe Nohi, raising a clenched fist in salutation.

"*Ranka ya dade*, Habe Nohi, Kai ne mai hikima. This day, you are victorious over the Nupe scoundrels who dared to invade us. All of Zazzau salutes your leadership."

"*Ranka ya dade*, Habe Nohi," the gathered crowd thundered in response, their voices in unison reverberating throughout the entire village.

Madaki Zaki bowed, as did his warrior companions and the members of the dancing troupe. Habe Nohi heartily acknowledged the customary felicitations with a wave of his hand. He praised Madaki Zaki and the Sojojin Zazzau for a battle well fought, and then declared that the celebrations should continue into the night.

As the vibrant dancing and drumming resumed, Nikitau eyed Habe Nohi enviously. The Habe did not notice his son-in-law. He was immersed in the celebrations, enjoying accolades and his people's adulation.

When the initial celebrations were concluded, the royal family exited the village square and additional festivities commenced with several additional drummer and dance troupes taking turns to entertain the people and extol the leadership of Habe Nohi and the might of the Sojojin Zazzau.

The Aftermath of Battle in Nupe: Five days Later

Dark clouds hovered in the sky, casting an ominous specter upon Nupeko – a village mourning the decimation of its warriors and nursing its wounded pride.

Thunder clapped, and lightning flashed, illuminating the darkening sky before plunging the village into gloom again. Soon enough, the bereaved clouds parted, allowing a torrent of rain and hail to empty upon the mournful village.

Inside Etsu Tsudi's palace, a desolate looking medicine man sat on the floor mat, his face a somber portrait of angst and anger. Majiya, the medicine man, scratched rough symbols with a chiseled rock onto a portion of bare earth where the raffia mat had been cut open for his work. He worked in a frenzy like a man possessed, all the while muttering to himself.

Etsu Tsudi was seated on his wooden throne, shifting impatiently as he awaited an explanation from Majiya as to why the ancestors had permitted Nupe to be humiliated in such a dreadful manner.

He tried to distract himself by looking around his palace, appreciating how much he had accomplished since he was a fugitive fleeing from his half-brothers in Idah.

His throne was decorated with amulets, beads, and cowrie shells. There were a few wooden stools and benches around his throne, all of which were empty now. The palace's inner mud walls were decorated with leopard and lion skin murals, and the palace floor was carpeted with a vast raffia mat.

On either side of Etsu Tsudi, armed guards stood like immovable statues, armed with gleaming machetes. Mokwa also stood beside the Etsu, observing Majiya's ritual as well.

Normally, Mokwa and the heads of the subordinate Nupe clans, Kusapa and Batachi, would have been seated on the stools around his throne. But Etsu Tsudi did not care for protocol today. He needed a quick and direct explanation from the ancestors.

As Etsu Tsudi continued looking around his palace, pain from the battle injury on his left shoulder shot through his side afresh, ending his temporary distraction. He shifted his weight to his right, easing pressure on his left shoulder which was now supported by a wrapper folded into a sling.

After what seemed like an unending session of unintelligible incantations, Majiya suddenly reached for a metal bowl beside him, emptied the ashes contained therein onto his shaved, charcoal-painted head and let out a shrill, agonized cry, clutching his bare chest as though he had been struck.

He looked up at his chagrined ruler, his eyes reddened from sorrow.

"Baghadozi Etsu Tsudi. My lord, our people say one should never sell a toothless dog to one's household lest the household be found unprotected in a time of need. We, proud people of this honorable land, have been sold a toothless dog by one of our own and we have been undone by this spineless act."

Etsu Tsudi's face darkened like the wailing clouds outside. His skin seemed taut on his long face, drawn by the frown that gripped his features.

"Who is it that has betrayed us, and how?" he demanded, his voice evidently pregnant with the rage that boiled within him.

"Tsowa, one of your three warrior chiefs," Majiya declared bluntly. "It was Tsowa who disobeyed the ancestors command to abstain from pleasures of the flesh with a woman the night before our battle. Alas, such insolence displeased the ancestors and cost us the battle. He must pay with his life for honor to be restored to our village."

Scarcely had Majiya finished proclaiming the guilty party than Etsu Tsudi was on his feet, his eyes ablaze with fury. He seized a sharp, gleaming machete from one of his guards and charged towards his palace entrance. The shocked guard, whose machete Etsu Tsudi had seized, recovered and followed his leader along with Mokwa and two other guards.

Outside, rain torrents lashed the earth. In front of the Etsu's arched palace entrance, beyond a few feet of elevated concrete verandah, the naked bodies of three shackled men trembled under the cruel rain.

These men knelt in the muddy soil, enduring the rain. Metal collars fastened around their necks were attached by chains to shackles around their wrists and ankles.

The three shackled men, Etsu Tsudi's chief warriors who had led the Nupe warriors to battle Zazzau, looked up, straining through the blur of the downpour to see who it was that had emerged from the Etsu's palace.

Etsu Tsudi's guards hurried to shield him from the rain with wide raffia mats used to fan the Etsu and other royal advisors on sweltering days. But Etsu Tsudi swatted the fans away, refusing in his anger to be shielded from the downpour.

Etsu Tsudi had arrested his chief warriors immediately after the battle. As warrior leaders, he held them accountable. Therefore, he had been punishing them daily since the defeat. Majiya's revelation now provided him with a single target upon whom he could unleash hell.

As Etsu Tsudi emerged before the chief warriors, two of them began to swear their innocence, praying that Majiya's divination would exonerate them of any foul play.

As Etsu Tsudi stepped closer to the men, his face freezing with menacing intent, the third man started to look like one who had just seen an apparition. His eyes engorged with terror and he trembled like a leaf in the stormy weather.

This man, Tsowa Edegi, began to beg and confess like a man possessed. He begged for mercy and beseeched the ancestors, who he assumed had revealed his disobedience to Majiya, to show mercy in exchange for his confession.

He confessed that that he had disobeyed Majiya's command from the ancestors. He had spent the night before with his two wives. Surely, his wives had cast a spell on him. He suggested they seduced him and coaxed him into believing his disobedience was trivial and would carry no dire consequences. He cursed them and hung his head.

Etsu Tsudi listened with exasperation to the babbling words of a man he had once considered a powerful warrior. When he had ordered his chief warriors apprehended after the defeat, he had not considered the possibility that one of these trusted warriors was solely responsible for Nupe's capitulation.

Tsowa, now quiet but still shaking with fear, looked up at the imposing figure of Etsu Tsudi who stood before him with a machete in hand. He glimpsed chilling visions of his imminent slaughter.

There was a swoosh as the machete blade slashed through air and rain. Then, a chopping sound as it struck flesh and bone. These sounds repeated rapidly, and two heads toppled in quick succession, landing with loud splashes in muddy puddles around Tsowa.

Blood erupted like fountains from the beheaded, bound bodies of Tsowa's colleagues. The bodies shuddered violently before collapsing to the puddled earth, releasing a flow of blood that combined with the dirty rain water all around Tsowa.

Tsowa bellowed as blood stung his eyes. He beheld the heads of his colleagues rolling in the mud like balls, their eyes engorged from sheer shock.

Tsowa was a battle-hardened warrior but the frenzy that now seized him obliterated any vestiges of courage. Seized with hysteria, he began another impassioned plea for mercy, crying as loudly as he could.

"Hold him!" Etsu Tsudi commanded.

The guards sprang into action, grabbing the struggling Tsowa in a vicelike grip by his shoulders and around his neck.

Etsu Tsudi stooped low and reached down between Tsowa's legs, his eyes never leaving the chief warrior's panicked eyes even for a moment.

As he raised the machete high, Tsowa realized what was about to occur and opened his mouth to scream but was stifled by one of the guard's palms which clasped across his mouth.

It happened very quickly.

One moment he had his manhood and the next it was in Etsu Tsudi's hands.

Tsowa's eyes rolled backwards as he felt the world around him begin to fade into oblivion. His horrified screaming reverberated through the village as he fell to the mud, released to his suffering by the guards who had hitherto restrained him.

Etsu Tsudi threw Tsowa's manhood down beside him like a rag cloth and spat on his body now unconscious, and bleeding in the rain.

Etsu Tsudi, his chest heaving from anger and from the intensity of his motions, glanced around at his guards and at Mokwa. They were all staring down at the slain bodies of the chief warriors. No one dared question the Etsu. They were all accustomed to his ruthlessness.

"Leave their bodies here in the rain to rot and be consumed by rats," Etsu Tsudi said, spitting out rain dripping into his mouth as he spoke.

"When the day breaks, gather all of Nupeko and our allied villages to witness this. Let this serve as a warning to anyone who dares to displease Etsu Tsudi or dares to disobey our ancestors."

CHAPTER SEVEN

The Animal in Nikitau

They are of kindred spirit, man and beast that prey on the weak and care for nothing but that which they seek

THEY STOOD IN EXTENDED rows of three, reaching farther than the eye could see. There were twenty thousand men poised for battle in the middle of the Zazzau training valley.

The warriors were armed with machetes, swords, spears, shields and archery. They wore metal helmets with nose, mouth, and eye slits. Behind the eye slits, steely eyes were visible – eyes brimming with feverish loyalty to Zazzau and consumed by a passion to live or die for their fearless leader, Habe Amina of Zazzau.

Amina sat on horseback at the focal point of the warrior's formation. Her headpiece was a large, purple Habe turban that stopped just above her ears, allowing her long braids to be visible down the sides of her slim, long face.

The turban was decorated with several ornaments and a large ruby gemstone at the forefront. Amina held the golden ornate staff that had been passed down by her grandfather in her right hand. She looked across her strong elite force with deep pride.

These special warriors, the Sojojin Bakwa, whom she named after her mother, had been carefully selected, and exceptionally trained in warfare by both Habe Amina and Madaki Zaki. They were fearless as the lions that protected their packs in the grassy plains of Zazzau.

Thinking of Madaki Zaki, Amina looked around to locate her trusted battle commander and mentor. He should have been on horseback right beside her or not far hence.

When she was unable to locate him at first try, she began to look farther out and around the valley. Where was Madaki Zaki? Why wouldn't he be here on this important eve of battle? Had something happened to him? She knew he would never desert her at such a critical moment. Something must have happened to him. She struggled to maintain her composure, lest she rattle her battle-ready warriors.

Amina called for Madaki Zaki, calmly at first. But her calls soon grew frantic. She willed her voice to carry as far as it could through the vast training valley. Suddenly it seemed to her that her voice was coming from somewhere foreign or somewhere outside of her. This strange turn heightened her worry and she called out louder.

Amina awoke abruptly in a cold sweat on her bed – an elevated platform of baked mud covered with a straw mat. She was stunned for a moment, her senses dulled by sleep and disoriented by the tease of a dream that had dominated her consciousness until now.

As her eyes grew accustomed to the darkness of her hut, her senses adjusted to the reality of the present. She could soon see the outlines of her mother's earthen pot, wooden stool, and a couple of calabashes with wooden utensils hanging off the front wall.

Amina observed the outline of her garments hanging from cords on the clay walls close to the entrance of a small inner chamber, her private room. She looked around, rubbing her eyes to dispel of all lingering sleep. She was alone, as expected. What had woken her? She wondered.

At that point she heard a sound, and she realized what it was that she heard – someone was in pain. The muffled cries were coming from her father's lower hut adjacent to the hut she had been asleep in. It was the hut her father shared with her mother whenever he required it. Amina now noticed that her mother was not on her baked-mud bed beside her.

Amina sprang from her bed. She reached under the straw mat spread across her mud-baked bed, searching until her hands grasped what she was looking for – the small carving dagger Madaki Zaki had given her for protection. With a few quick steps, she was out of her hut and darted as fast as she could towards her father's nearby dwelling.

Amina reached her father's lower hut in little more than an instant and crouched by the entrance, hiding behind the outside wall and peering within.

The half-moon high in the sky provided just enough light for her to see into her father's hut. What she saw hurt like a blow to the stomach and dropped her to her knees, angry tears stinging her now wide-open eyes.

Her mother laid naked and spread eagled with her back on the bare earth floor of her husband's hut. She was immobilized, pressed down at her wrists and ankles by Nikitau. Her mouth was partially covered by his large, dirty right palm and, her face was turned towards the entrance of the hut, away from his naked body as he gyrated atop her.

Amina heard her father's hateful words almost spat into her mother's face. "Give me a male child, woman. This is what you want, isn't it? This is what you need to give me a male child!"

Amina gripped her carving dagger and began to rise, anger and horror combining to extinguish all fear. She loathed her father. She would stab him until she was certain he would never be able to harm her mother again.

Amina's eyes suddenly locked with her mother's and she saw a look of alarm leap into her mother's teary eyes, focusing on Amina's hand which was now raised high with the pointed end of her dagger end visible in the moonlight.

Amina took a quiet step forward. Her mother began to shake her head as vigorously as she could under her husband's weight. Amina tried to argue with her eyes, no words. She narrowed her eyes and bit her lower lip to hold back tears, but the tears spilled anyway and flowed freely down her cheeks.

Princess Bakwa mouthed the word "no" and then, she began to gyrate as best she could in rhythm to her husband's rough movements.

Amina wondered why the sudden change. What was she doing? Perhaps she was pretending it was consensual to deter Amina from interfering? Or perhaps she had plunged herself into deep recesses of denial, giving herself to her husband even though he had initially taken her by force.

Either way, this was despicable, and Amina was horrified to think that her mother could only cope with this if she pretended this assault was not rape. How could a husband rape his wife?

Amina continued to look upon her mother's face. She saw a look of anguish and shame. This was too much to bear. Amina either had to attack or leave. She paused, debating with her dagger still held high. Her heartbeat galloped like a stampede of frightened cattle and her stomach had knotted so tight that it hurt. She felt a lump rise to her throat.

Nikitau, grunting, remained oblivious to Amina's presence by the door.

Amina dropped her hand and slowly forced herself to turn around. She raced back to her mother's hut, still biting her lower lip to keep from yelling out in agony. When she reached the hut, she collapsed breathless on the dirt floor and surrendered to an earthquake of sorrow.

CHAPTER EIGHT

Seeds of Alliance

He who says he does not need an ally must be prepared to suffer a great loss

THE NEXT DAY WAS, to most people in Zazzau, no different than the day before. Nomadic herdsmen led their cattle out to green pastures while fishermen proceeded to River Kaduna in hopes that the river would yield its treasures of fine fish that swam deep within.

The village women catered to all manners of domestic concerns and their children played in the dusty streets. The village elders were considered too weak to work and too wise to cook. So, they settled in basking spots under shady trees long before the sun was high, ready to surpass the prior day's efforts at doing absolutely nothing.

But for Amina, the next day felt sadly different than the one before. She had awoken from a fitful sleep hoping that the rape she witnessed had been a dream.

But it was too real for her mind to have conjured it. She sat for a long time on her bed, arms folded around raised knees with her head buried in her knees. She rocked herself gently back and forth, bleeding silent tears from an injured heart.

Soon her mother called for her. When she reached her mother, Amina found that she could not bring herself to meet her eyes. No words were spoken in the initial moments. The horrific events of the night before hung between them like a thick fog.

Amina knew better than to speak of the act and Princess Bakwa found some semblance of dignity in pretending the act never occurred. And so, it was that a fractured normalcy soon resumed between them.

Princess Bakwa informed Amina that the Habe had decided to journey to Katsina for a matter of strategic importance and had asked her to prepare a generous gift for Sarki Ibrahim Maje, the ruler of Katsina.

She needed Amina to go ask her grandfather whether he would prefer to take a full herd of cows as his gift or a combination of cows and goats.

Amina set on her task right away, walking the short distance from her mother's area of the palace courtyard to the Habe's palace courts. As she walked, her head hung low. Should she tell grandfather? She wanted to. Her father deserved to be severely punished for his heinous actions.

But her mother would likely not want Habe Nohi to learn of it. The embarrassment would be too much for her to bear. Amina felt hot tears roll down her cheeks.

Pull yourself together Amina, she thought. *You are stronger than this.*

She walked on, kicking pebbles in frustration. What possesses a man to think he has a right to a woman's body? That he can take her without her consent? Because he is physically stronger? Because societal hierarchy has permitted him? She bit her lower lip in frustration and silently vowed to reverse this cruel normalcy for Zazzau women. She vowed she would never, ever, be subordinate to any man.

When Amina arrived at the palace, Habe Nohi was seated on his throne in consult with his council of noble men on matters of strategic alliances and village security.

Lawan Shehu, the village head, had an earnest look in his frog-wide eyes. He leaned forward on his stool, gathering his flowing robes up to his ankles so that he would not step on them as he shifted his weight.

"*Ranka ya dade* Habe Nohi," he began with a typical respectful salutation. "Our people say when clouds gather and darken, they never disperse until they have emptied their bowels.

Although we successfully repelled those Nupe mosquitoes with a great show of might, we must ready ourselves for a retaliation. The dark clouds of war have gathered, and I am certain Etsu Tsudi will return for vengeance with a force ten times stronger. We must warn our people and warriors to remain vigilant."

Alkatin Aliyu, the chief judge, was seated on the opposite side of Lawan Shehu at the foot of the Habe. He had been staring at the polished stone floor but now looked up. He had a look of disapproval darkening his wizened features.

"Lawan Shehu, do not be so small minded as to think that our Habe is ignorant of the threat or naïve about how to keep our people safe. Your counsel related to the people's pulse is valued but it must be tempered with appropriate words that demonstrate trust of our Habe's wisdom and judgment."

Lawan Shehu recoiled like a viper treaded upon. He opened his mouth to respond but did not get a chance to defend himself.

Habe Nohi quelled the budding argument with a wave of his hand. "Be calm, my noble counselors. I have indeed heard rumors that Etsu Tsudi persists in his quest to conquer Zazzau and indeed all Hausaland.

Our scouts also say he is planning to build a mighty confederacy across all ten Nupe clans. If he succeeds, I concede we stand no chance alone. However, the solution lies not in promoting a sense of unease among our people but rather in building strategic alliances across our beloved Hausaland.

We must outmaneuver Etsu Tsudi in strategy and be prepared to overwhelm him with a superior warrior force when the time comes. I have a plan."

Habe Nohi paused for a moment to allow his words sink. Then, he continued.

"I plan to journey soon to visit our brethren in Katsina, to seek an alliance with Sarki Ibrahim Maje. This alliance, I hope, will be the first of six alliances that will unite all seven villages of Hausaland in trade and war.

Surely, there will be resistance. As you all know, Sarki Ibrahim Maje and Sarki Muhammed Kosoki of Kano are fierce rivals and likely will not want to ally. But we must find a way to remind them how an isolated broom twig becomes much more valuable when bound with other twigs to sweep a yard clean."

Habe Nohi's council of nobles began to speak to one another, approving of the direction Habe Nohi had presented. Habe Nohi leaned back in his chair, attentive to the ensuing dialog. Amina had been standing by the palace side door, observing and listening to the proceedings. Though her heart remained heavy, her mind was clear. She was always eager to gain an understanding of village royal affairs whenever presented with the opportunity.

The nobles discussed how Katsina and Kano had always been rivals for supremacy and control of the trade route to Cairo. Thus, it would undoubtedly be difficult to get the leaders to ally.

They praised Habe Nohi's strategy to target an alliance with Katsina, the comparatively weaker and smaller village, first. Once the first alliance was established, it would be clear to Sarki Muhammed Kosoki of Kano that, given the alliance of Zazzau and Katsina, he no longer enjoyed a dominant position of trade and military resources.

The nobles surmised that Habe Nohi was banking on the fact that Sarki Muhammed Kosoki would be convinced to join the budding alliance, so Kano could retain its relative importance in the region.

The council of nobles ventured into lofty discussions of a future united Hausaland.

It would be a Hausa Bakwai empire just like Bayajidda, the ancient founder of Hausaland, had always desired. They recounted the legend of Zazzau and the six other Hausa villages.

The legend held that once upon a time now long forgotten, Bayajidda, son of an ancient king of Baghdad, was forced to journey westward from his home towards Africa. His forced sojourn through the Sahara was because of a falling out with his father and consequent banishment.

During his travels, Bayajidda happened upon a desolate people impeded by a mysterious snake, from access to water in their village well. Bayajidda felt compassion for the people and bravely battled the snake, eventually killing it.

In return, the queen of the desolate townsfolk gave him her hand in marriage and the people declared him king. Bayajidda's six offspring with the queen and a seventh with a second wife became the founders of the seven Hausa villages called Hausa *Bakwai*. These villages were Daura, Katsina, Zazzau, Gobir, Kano, Rano, and Biram.

After extended discussions amongst themselves, the council of nobles finally quieted down.

"Habe Nohi, *Mai Hikima*," Alkatin Aliyu now addressed Habe Nohi. "As always, your wisdom is supreme and your counsel like fresh breeze on a beautiful morning.

We remain at your service; ready to discuss how we can ensure a successful alliance and ready to accompany you on this great quest when the time comes."

The other noble men nodded in agreement.

Habe Nohi acknowledged their support with thanks.

"I have a plan that will guarantee a successful alliance and will disclose it when the time is right. Given how important this alliance is, it is absolutely imperative that we pursue every angle to ensure success."

Habe Nohi concluded his meeting with the nobles. As they exited the palace, Amina approached her grandfather to deliver her mother's message.

Habe Nohi, seated on his throne, listened to the message his granddaughter had come to deliver all the while observing her downcast countenance with some concern. When she was finished speaking, he told her he would prefer to take a combination of the best cows and goats in Zazzau to Katsina. He would spare no expense towards ensuring a successful alliance.

Her task accomplished, Amina curtsied to her grandfather and turned to go.

Habe Nohi stopped her. He ushered her closer, prompting her to sit at the foot of his throne just as she had done so many times since she was a little girl.

"Come sit on this stool next to me, my little butterfly, and tell me what matter is so great that it clouds your beautiful young face."

Amina turned around and began walking towards her grandfather. She dared not look up. Her emotions thrashed within her like unsettled snakes clustered in a pit.

She was too sad to even begin to contemplate telling her grandfather about the rape. Nikitau was her father and her mother's husband after all. No one would believe it and her mother would probably deny that it ever occurred. Amina's short walk to the footstool near her grandfather's throne felt like a thousand steps.

Amina reached the throne but rather than sit on the footstool, she climbed up the few steps leading to Habe Nohi's throne and threw her arms around him, burying her forehead in the small of his neck.

She had assumed this posture so many times as a little girl. Her grandfather had been like a father to her and had always carved out time to tell her legendary Zazzau stories when she was little.

Often, she would fall asleep in his lap while listening to him detail one legend of Zazzau or the other. Sometimes, he would have a servant carry her back to her mother's hut. Other times, he would have a servant lay her to sleep on a cotton-cushioned raffia mat at the foot of his own bed.

"I would really like to accompany you on your journey to Katsina, grandfather. I was sad because I know you have official matters to attend to and would not want me there as a distraction." Amina fabricated this request as an excuse for her sadness. But there was some truth to her request as well for she longed for an opportunity to someday visit all villages in Hausaland.

Habe Nohi returned his granddaughter's hug and patted her back. "I am overjoyed with your request actually. It is very pleasing to me and aligns with my plans for you."

Amina perked up. "What plans?"

Habe Nohi smiled and touched the tip of her nose with his finger. "That's for me to know for sure. But you can be certain, my plans for you are the best possible plans."

Amina wanted to pry further but decided against it. Her mother's predicament was enough to worry about now. She leaned her head onto Habe Nohi's shoulder.

"*Haba Amina?*" Habe Nohi said, gently lifting her head from his shoulder so he could look into her eyes. "How could my beautiful little butterfly ever be a distraction to me? You are an inspiration, not a distraction my dear. Of course, you are welcome to accompany me. I'm sure you will learn a great many things on this journey."

Amina felt her lips curl into a smile. Despite her sadness, her heart warmed with gratitude for his words. The journey to Katsina would indeed provide an exciting opportunity to understand more royal matters. The time away from home might also help take her mind off the evil she had witnessed.

Amina threw her arms around her grandfather and hugged him tight again. Grandfather Nohi was the only reason she could believe that perhaps not all men were beastly creatures.

She wished now, as she had done so many times before, that he was her father. But she reminded herself to be grateful to her ancestors that she had him in her life in some way. She could scarcely think what she would do when he eventually passed on to the realm of the ancestors.

'*Ranka ya dade Habe Nohi Mai Hikima,*" one of the palace guards at the entrance called out in a loud voice. "A villager and his family are waiting in the palace courtyard, sir. They are humbly seeking an audience with you. This villager says he owes your granddaughter a profound debt for saving his daughter's life. He has come here today with his wife and daughter to pledge his daughter's devotion to your granddaughter."

Amina looked up in surprise and smiled. She had not thought about Aisha or her family since saving her from Mustapha. She had been too occupied with her own family issues.

A man dressed in a simple blue loincloth and a white cotton vest walked into the palace and across the palace hallway toward Habe Nohi's throne. He was accompanied by a woman and a young girl each wearing a simple, multi-patterned wrapper knotted across the chest.

The man and his family laid prostrate before Habe Nohi upon reaching the throne. While the man raised his head to utter fervent salutations to his ruler, the women remained in silent reverence with their foreheads to the ground.

Habe Nohi raised his right hand in acknowledgment of their salutations. One of his guards commanded that the family rise and state their business before the Habe.

Amina smiled at Aisha who returned the smile as her father began to state their business.

"Habe Nohi, my name is Idris. I am a humble carpenter. This is my wife Laila and my eldest daughter Aisha. We live in the southeast corridor of the village. We are grateful that the ancestors have blessed Zazzau with your leadership."

Habe Nohi nodded and smiled. He bid him continue.

"I am sure you have by now been informed of the inspiring courage her royal highness, your granddaughter showed in rescuing my daughter here from that criminal Mustapha who sought to steal her virtue in such a horrible manner.

We are not here to demand justice as we trust that you in your wisdom will surely mete out the punishment that animal deserves. We are here on a more noble cause which Aisha here will speak of should she be permitted to speak in your presence."

Aisha waited for the Habe's permission and upon dispensing customary salutations, she turned to Amina.

"Your royal highness, my esteemed princess. When you saved me the other day, I was too shocked to properly express how grateful I was..." she paused and looked down. She then continued.

"I mean, how grateful I am for your bravery. We have come here today with gifts of flock and chickens, with as much as we peasants can afford."

Aisha paused again, then looked up at Amina with earnest eyes.

"Princess Amina, you are my hero now and forever. Indeed, if it were possible to for me to capture all the words on the lips of every person in this village and use them to declare my gratitude to you, I would still fall short in expressing myself to you. Beyond the gift of flock and chickens, my parents and I would like to offer you something far more precious and would be honored if you would accept it."

Aisha at this point dropped to her knees, her earnest eyes still fixed on Amina.

"My princess, I ask that you accept me into your father's household as one of your loyal servants. I pledge that I will serve you and defend you faithfully with my life should I ever be required to lay it down for you, as you were willing to do for me."

Amina's eyes grew large. When she helped Aisha the other day, it had been to her, merely an involuntary action. It was the right thing to do. She looked to her grandfather, her eyes seeking searching his for an appropriate reaction.

Habe Nohi smiled. He addressed Aisha and her parents.

"Aisha, you are obviously a bright young woman. Amina would be delighted to have you join her parents' household in service to her. In honor of your sacrifice, I will allow your parents to return to their household with double the gifts they have brought here. Today, my household has gained a devoted servant. But I assure you, Idris, that you have not lost a daughter to us."

Grandfather always knows the right things to say, Amina thought.

As Idris again began to thank Habe Nohi, Amina studied Aisha's face for any signs of coercion. She would not accept if she suspected that Aisha was being forced to do this against her will. But all Amina saw was a happy girl, overjoyed that she had been accepted into the royal household as Amina's handmaid.

CHAPTER NINE

The Exploitation of Princess Bakwa

The measure of one's success or failure is that line beyond which one is unwilling to proceed

PRINCESS BAKWA OPENED HER eyes. She blinked, straining her mind to recognize her unfamiliar surroundings and to dispel the panic that suddenly seized her.

Where am I, she wondered, slowly pulling herself up to a sitting position upon what she recognized to be a rock. She could see the giant orange sun setting in the distance across a horizon of tall grass and a clustered variety of trees.

The evening was close to dissolving into night, just as it had been when she had gone to visit Mai Sihiri, the Zazzau village sorcerer, earlier. That visit was the last thing she remembered prior to gaining consciousness here.

She looked around nervously, observing that all around her was foliage, tall grass, and trees. She realized that she was no longer in Zazzau. The sound of nearby rushing waters drew her attention and she angled her head in the direction of the gushing white waterfalls cascading over an expanse of rocks a few feet away.

A cool breeze slapped the surface of the waterfall and she felt a cold mist as water droplets wafted with the wind onto her bare shoulders. She reached down to pull up her wrapper which was draped across her chest and knotted securely below her armpits.

"Where am I?" she asked, speaking to no one in particular. She could hardly hear herself think louder than her pounding heart. She strained to remember how she had come to be in this place, wherever it was.

"You are in Kamuku forest at the Dogon Ruwa waterfall."

The voice was calm and precise. She recognized the voice and turned to see Mai Sihiri, the wiry old Zazzau village sorcerer sitting atop another rock behind her with his legs folded under him and his right hand massaging his long, white beard.

His small beady eyes were calm, almost meditative. Princess Bakwa had never felt so relieved as she did upon seeing Mai Sihiri. It did not matter how she had come to be in Kamuku forest. Mai Sihiri was here with her and the ancestors were always with him. So, all must be well.

"What are we doing here, Mai Sihiri?" Princess Bakwa asked, shivering from the cold caress of the waterfall droplets.

"This is the will of the ancestors, my child. We are in the place they have commanded that you should come to if your request is to be granted. You are to proceed to the base of the waterfall and state the desires of your heart just as you said to me back in my home moments ago. Once you do that, they will provide additional instructions. This is the will of the ancestors."

Princess Bakwa did not hesitate. She had many questions swirling in her head. But she was focused on satisfying the reason for her secret visit to Mai Sihiri.

She lifted her wrapper above her knees to allow flexibility to leap off the rock upon which she sat. She wore snake skin slippers with sandal straps that fitted tightly around her ankles. She was grateful for the protection the fitted slippers provided as she imagined the wet rocks at the base of the waterfall would be slippery.

The walk to the base of the waterfall was a short one. As she walked, she was aware that Mai Sihiri followed behind.

Princess Bakwa soon reached the thrashing torrents of the waterfall. She moved closer, picking out a path of wet but stable rocks visible in the expansive stream that had formed at the foot of the torrents.

She got as close as she possibly could to the raging waters without being in danger of being swallowed by the deluge. Then, she carefully positioned her footing on a flat rock with a wide base before allowing her full weight onto it.

She turned around to face Mai Sihiri who had also stopped on a flat rock quite close to her and was now standing still, leaning on the tall wooden staff he depended upon to move his old bones.

Princess Bakwa tried to decipher Mai Sihiri's serene expression but his wrinkled face was void of emotion and his eyes were shut. He was under the influence of the ancestors, she concluded.

Her eyes spoke. What now?

The Dogon Ruwa waterfall dropped over a steep rocky cliff. The cascading waters bouncing off the waterfall's rocky backdrop behind Princess Bakwa were splashing onto her and starting to soak her wrapper.

She could taste the salinity of the waterfall and smell the musty odors emanating from the wet rocks upon which the waters continuously fell.

Princess Bakwa now felt she had gotten too close and started to move away to avoid getting thoroughly soaked but froze when Mai Sihiri ordered her to stop in a rather stern voice. His eyes remained shut but he bared his broken, dirty teeth in a momentary flash of anger.

"Do not leave the spot where you stand! Speak to the ancestors now. Repeat your request as loudly as you can three times."

Princess Bakwa swallowed hard. Mai Sihiri had startled her. Slightly disoriented, she proclaimed as loudly as she could over the rumble of the waterfall,

"Oh, most gracious ancestors of mine. Please look upon me with mercy and grant me a male child. From the union of my husband Nikitau and I, please grant me a male child."

She repeated these words three times as loudly as she could then cast her eyes back to Mai Sihiri.

What now?

Mai Sihiri's eyes remained tightly shut in meditation.

Princess Bakwa waited. Her wet wrapper was beginning to cling to her body. She looked down upon herself, feeling embarrassment set in. She wore a flimsy white undergarment slip underneath her wrapper. But the undergarment was not enough to hide her body now starting to be exposed by the clinging of the wet wrapper to her body.

Princess Bakwa could feel her nipples stiffening underneath. She raised her hands and folded them across her chest in a desperate effort to retain some modesty. She was shivering. Mai Sihiri finally opened his eyes and spoke. "Take your clothes off."

Princess Bakwa's eyes widened in shock and disbelief. No, this could not be happening. She began to move away from the waterfall, shaking her head.

"I will do no such thing."

"You made a request of the ancestors. There is a process that must be followed, Princess Bakwa. Our ancestors have commanded that I rub your womb with mud from these falls and cleanse you from the crown of your head to the soles of your feet with its waters. These are the necessary steps for you to conceive a male child."

Princess Bakwa bowed her head, feeling completely helpless and embarrassed. Another shiver ran through her as the evening breeze again swept over her. This could not be happening.

But even as she considered how detestable her current predicament was, she recalled she had gone to Mai Sihiri knowing she would have to sacrifice something.

She had expected that the ancestors would require an offering of a goat or two. Perhaps some chickens too. She had expected she might have to drink the blood of an animal or cut her hand in blood sacrifice. These were all rituals she had heard about from others who had requested similar favors from the ancestors.

What if Mai Sihiri decided to do more than just rub his filthy hands all over her body? She shuddered, not from the cold, but from the thought of Mai Sihiri's shriveled old hands running over her naked body.

Why couldn't she wash herself? Why would the ancestors ask him to do it? She looked up at him, trying to decipher if he had an ulterior motive.

If Mai Sihiri was excited about the prospect of running his hands all over her supple body, the sorcerer did not show it. He remained focused on her, steely-eyed and almost unblinking, awaiting her decision.

Hot tears filled her eyes. Such a disgusting old man, she thought, her body now trembling with muted range.

A sober nod was all she could muster with her head still bowed in shame, and tears streaming down her cheeks and onto her lips. Her soul wailed but her lips could only tremble in sorrow.

Mai Sihiri did unto her what he said the ancestors had requested. He performed his task in a dutiful, almost perfunctory manner.

But when his task was complete, he stared at Princess Bakwa's beautiful, supple body laid bare and submissive before him on the waterfall base where he had washed her. Her eyes were shut. Apart from her shivers, she appeared restful.

Princess Bakwa could feel Mai Sihiri observing her. She felt violated by the thought of his eyes roaming over her body. She longed to cover herself, but her desire for a male child restrained her. Mai Sihiri was the village sorcerer, sworn to celibacy and dedicated to the ancestors. *Was he no different than other feeble men unable to restrain their sexual desires?*

Amina wondered if he was still performing the ritual. But she dismissed the consideration. She knew his task was done once he took his hands off her body, once she sensed his eyes pouring over her.

"I have not been with a woman since I was a very young man. But I must do as the ancestors command. We must obey them, so they may grant your desire." Mai Sihiri said in a low voice, fueled by desire.

Princess Bakwa's eyes flew open. She thought to break away from him, but her desire for a male child restrained her once more. *Did he say this was the will of the ancestors?*

Mai Sihiri was already kissing her. First, he kissed her forehead, then her neck. When she did not resist, he began to explore her body, kissing her shoulders and then moving down to her breasts. Princess Bakwa did not resist as she felt him lower himself onto her.

She kept her eyes shut and cast her mind somewhere to a time when she was a little girl playing in her Baba's palace courtyard. Once she decided to allow Mai Sihiri to touch her, she had resigned herself to the realization that he might take advantage of her.

If this was what was required for her to conceive a male heir who would, in due course, rule Zazzau with the full respect and privileges afforded to any male Habe, then so be it. Far be it from her to question the price of favor requested from the ancestors.

But, if Mai Sihiri was merely taking advantage of her for his own lustful satisfaction, then may the ancestors punish him dearly for this heinous act committed in their name.

The cry in Princess Bakwa's heart soon sounded loud on her lips. Her heartfelt petition for justice resounded as a desperate cry for help. Tears streamed down her cheeks as her apprehensive eyeballs moved behind her closed eyelids. Her lips quivered and, her entire body shook, ravaged by the distress she felt deep within.

As she struggled to somehow accept that which she had succumbed to, she felt a hand touch her shoulder. She retracted from the touch, falling backwards like she had just been stung by a bee.

At that moment, her eyes opened, and she saw that she had not moved from her position all evening. She was not by the waterfall in Kamuku forest.

Rather, she was seated in Mai Sihiri's dwelling with her legs folded under her in a meditative stance. Mai Sihiri, who had just touched her on the shoulder, was seated across from her and watching her intently.

There was a small fire crackling between them. Next to the fire, spread out on rock-punctuated earth, was an assemblage of cowries, smooth stones and little bird skulls which Mai Sihiri had employed for the incantation required to connect Princess Bakwa to the ancestors.

Princess Bakwa shrank even further from him and alarmingly ran her hands over her body, feeling for wetness from the waterfall which had felt so very real only a moment ago. She was dry as a withered leaf in the dry Harmattan season.

How could this be? she wondered. Her mouth dropped open and her eyes widened in disbelief, locking with Mai Sihiri's eyes and demanding an explanation.

"What is it, my child?" Mai Sihiri asked. Princess Bakwa noted that he was dry as a desert. His searching eyes betrayed no knowledge of anything contrary to what was evident between them both.

Princess Bakwa shut her mouth and her eyes, shaking her head vigorously like one trying to dispel a bothersome vision. Had she imagined or dreamed what happened? It had all felt so real. She could still feel his rough, wrinkled hands on her body, roughly prodding her private parts. She shuddered at the memory, if she could call it that.

"My child, did the ancestors reveal to you if they would grant your request?"

Princess Bakwa rose, gathering her wrapper around her. She needed to be anywhere but near Mai Sihiri at this moment. "Yes," she said with a slight stutter, her eyes averted from his. "I must go now."

Mai Sihiri watched expressionless as Princess Bakwa exited. When she was gone, he exhaled before angrily slapping his elemental incantation objects away, sending the items flying into the fire and beyond.

"What have I done?" he lamented. "Why have I allowed himself succumb so cheaply to lustful desires?"

He crashed his forehead to the dusty earth and began wailing, beseeching the ancestors to forgive his overstep and nullify any consequences.

CHAPTER TEN

Seeking the Ancestors' Will

Whatsoever will be, will be. Or will it?

IT WAS DARK. ZAZZAU villagers were asleep, and even the moon was gone this night. However, one man, like a ghost in the night, was making his way to the back of the village, guided by a flaming wick on a short stave.

Zazzau was situated at the foot of several sandy and rocky hills. Its many mud dwellings, like elongated roots that emanated from the base of the hills, were spread wide across the dusty plain below the hills. On the left side of the hill base, at an elevated point, was a large cavern with enough room to fit several Zazzau households.

The solitary figure carefully ascended a few stepping stones leading to the mouth of the cavern. He knew the path, so his short climb was facile, even in the dark

At the mouth of the cavern, the figure, Habe Nohi, stood still and waved his flaming stave. He repeated this motion three times, then waited to be permitted entry. He had waited as late as he could, so he could make this visit without his guards, and undetected by anyone.

Ordinarily, he would summon Mai Sihiri or have one of his servants carry a message to Mai Sihiri. But for matters as important as this one was, Habe Nohi wanted a private audience. This quest, he believed, was crucial to the long-term survival of Zazzau.

A grating noise sounded as a small boulder that secured the entrance to the cavern was pushed aside ever so slightly. A wrinkled hand emerged from the cavern opening and bid him enter.

Inside the cavern was a vast area aglow with several flaming wicks on tall staves. Beside each flaming stave was a metal rod capped with a dry human skull, and littered at the base of each metal rod, was an assortment of dry human and animal bones.

There was a slow burning fire in the middle of the room. But for the crackling of the fire as its flames pulsated, all was quiet within the cavern.

Behind the crackling fire, Mai Sihiri was seated on a small wooden stool with one hand on his shaved head and the other massaging his long, white beard. His shoulders were hunched underneath a dark robe.

Though Mai Sihiri's wrinkled face looked like it had lived too many decades on borrowed time, his small beady eyes told a different story altogether. His eyes were youthful and alive like the flames that danced before him. They portrayed his youthful spirit gifted to him by Zazzau's ancestors to whom he was spiritually connected.

Habe Nohi removed the woolly blanket he had wrapped around his body and head to provide warmth from the cold Harmattan outside. When he reached the fire, he sat on the bare floor opposite the sorcerer, crossing his legs under him.

"*Ranka ya dade* Habe Nohi," the shrunken sorcerer greeted in a gruff voice. He wore a necklace of cowries, dried bird skulls and long animal canines. He now shifted his hand off his beard to massage his necklace but closed his eyes and maintained his meditative stance.

"*Ranka ya dade*, Mai Sihiri," Habe Nohi replied.

"My esteemed Habe. I know you would not be here by yourself at this time unless this is an urgent matter. How can I be of service?"

"Mai Sihiri, the matter I have brought to you is of paramount importance to the future of Zazzau. Zazzau has been violated once and I cannot allow that to happen again."

Mai Sihiri's eyes fell open. He squeezed his jaws and lips tight to hold back from saying something then shut his eyes again. Habe Nohi noticed this and wondered why his demeanor changed. But he chose to focus on his mission instead.

Mai Sihiri spoke in a small voice, halting voice. "Who...er...how has Zazzau been violated? Is everyone in the royal family alright? Princess Bakwa, Princess Amina, Nikitau?"

Habe Nohi glared at him and nodded impatiently. *Why wouldn't they be?* He wondered if he had Mai Sihiri's complete attention. Perhaps the sorcerer was still meditating, focused elsewhere.

"Yes Mai Sihiri, of course they are fine. What I mean is that Etsu Tsudi violated our land and our people. We won but we lost many warriors. When he attacks again, I must ensure to inflict such a crushing defeat on him that he will never again imagine journeying up north."

Mai Sihiri's eyes flew open again but this time with a childlike twinkle.

Again, Habe Nohi observed his change of mood. This time, he blurted out. "What is going on with you, Mai Sihiri? One moment you looked concerned and the next you seem excited. If this is not a good time for discussion, I could return later."

Mai Sihiri laughed and exhaled with relief. He relaxed his stance.

"No, my esteemed Habe. This is a good time to discuss. I was initially concerned because it seemed the ancestors were indicating your visit was related to a family issue, a violation of some sort. But now, I understand better. It would appear there is nothing amiss. Please accept my apologies and proceed."

Habe Nohi studied Mai Sihiri. "Now I am getting worried. Are you certain the ancestors are not, as you say, trying to communicate a family issue?"

Mai Sihiri nodded and laughed again, dismissing the notion and reassuring Habe Nohi that all was well.

Assured, Habe Nohi proceeded to outline the reason for his visit. A visibly relieved Mai Sihiri now listened to him with rapt attention.

"Okay, I have come to you seeking confirmation from the ancestors that an alliance with Katsina is the right move to boost our military strength. To seal this alliance, I plan to propose a gesture of marriage between my granddaughter and Sarki Ibrahim Maje. For such a proposal, I need the blessing of our ancestors."

Mai Sihiri opened his mouth to speak but suddenly convulsed. His pupils vanished into the back of his head, revealing only the white of his eyes.

Habe Nohi fell backwards. He had seen Mai Sihiri perform many kinds of oddities when connecting to the ancestral realm but until now, any connection to the ancestral connection would occur more gradually. This time, the connection had occurred quite unexpectedly.

CHAPTER ELEVEN

The Will of the Ancestors

*He who relies on an interpreter must be prepared
to sacrifice some meaning*

MAI SIHIRI SUDDENLY FELT cold, colder than the feel of an icy river's touch on a frigid Harmattan morning. He shivered, rubbing his shoulders to muster whatever warmth he could. He was surrounded by fog so thick, he could almost reach out and grab it.

Mai Sihiri recognized this milieu and fell, remaining reverent with his hands at full stretch. When he lifted his head, incantations and praises for the ancestors began to pour out of him, his body trembling in rhythm to his intonation. Like his trembling body, his mind agitated like chaotic waves lashing out at a sandy shore. Why had he been summoned here so suddenly?

When Habe Nohi showed up at his dwelling, he assumed that Princess Bakwa must have reported what he did to her. Although she had awoken in his cavern, mystified as to what occurred, she could have figured out later that he transported her to the forest and assaulted her.

Once she examined her body at home, she would have discovered evidence. Although fearful of dire consequences, Mai Sihiri had steeled his resolve, prepared to deny any accusations from Habe Nohi. He had been relieved to learn that Habe Nohi had not come to accuse him. But now that he had been summoned by the ancestors, that relief evaporated.

They knew the truth!

The fog around Mai Sihiri shifted, swirling to form myriads of shapes like clouds adrift in the sky. Soon, the fog began to move rapidly, morphing into conjoined, faceless human forms. These ancestral forms appeared and fizzled almost immediately like flashes of starlight manifesting and vanishing in a night sky.

From deep within the foggy, faceless ancestors, guttural utterances like the rumble of provoked waters sounded. Many voices spoke at once like a chattering cacophony incomprehensible to the untrained ear.

Mai Sihiri stilled himself and listened hard with his trained ear, searching for understanding of their unified utterances.

"Mai Sihiri, our trusted mouthpiece, guardian of Zazzau's ancestral pathway. If you who are trusted and favored wish to retain our favor, you must face the consequences of your actions." Mai Sihiri felt a stab of panic pierce his heart. He began to shake his head and plead for mercy.

"My beloved ancestors, far be it from me to question your counsel, wisdom, or judgment. For you reside in realms beyond our simple human world and comprehend all things spirit and human.

However, I humbly ask that you show mercy to your devoted servant. If Habe Nohi ever finds out what I have done to his daughter, he will surely end my life. Please, I beg of you, permit me to remain your humble servant on earth a while longer."

Mai Sihiri bowed his head to the earth. His body trembled even more now, wrapped in the cruel embrace of cold and fear.

There was silence for an extended period. The ancestral shapes continued to swirl, to morph and fizzle like ghostly illusions materializing and then vaporizing into the atmosphere.

Finally, the rumbling voices declared.

"We have heard your plea for mercy Mai Sihiri, our devoted mouthpiece. But we also hear the broken heart of Princess Bakwa, whom you violated, calling for justice.

Where there is mercy there must also justice. We therefore declare that no man shall judge you but the Habe himself. If the Habe does not judge you, neither shall we nor any other man judge you."

How was this justice tempered with mercy? His fate in Habe Nohi's hands, the hands of the father whose daughter he violated? He began to speak quickly, desperate hoping the ruling he had just heard was not the final word.

"My beloved ancestors! Please forgive me if I am too bold in testing the limits of your mercy and graciousness. But Habe Nohi will show no mercy, of this I am certain. Surely, there must be another way. I beg of you!"

Thunder boomed in the sky, sending reverberations all around.

Mai Sihiri recoiled like a snail taking refuge under its shell.

"Do not test our patience!" the rumbling voices bellowed. "We could and should end your life for what you have done. We could and should turn the hearts of every villager in Zazzau against you so that they seek only to destroy you.

But we have not done these things. Instead, we have placed your judgment solely in the hands of the father of the daughter you violated. And you dare question the limits of our mercy?"

Mai Sihiri began to apologize and to thank the ancestors for their wisdom and mercy.

"You will return to the Habe Nohi now, Mai Sihiri. We have heard his request concerning the alliance with Katsina. This is our word where that is concerned: The alliance with Katsina is good and will serve Zazzau well. But his intention to betroth Amina to Sarki Ibrahim Maje is bad. If he proceeds down that path, it will be the end of him."

Mai Sihiri could scarcely believe what he just heard. He blurted out his thoughts.

"But how will the betrothal be the end of Habe Nohi? What must he do differently to secure this beneficial alliance?"

"Go now Mai Sihiri," the voices rumbled. The rumbling was softer now, starting to fade. "Return to Habe Nohi. You have been with us long enough."

Suddenly, Mai Sihiri found himself back in his cavern. As his vision returned and the familiar environs of his cavern registered, he perceived Habe Nohi still seated opposite from him, looking expectant and anxious.

"How long was I gone for?" Mai Sihiri asked in a dry, tired voice. He tried to dissimulate his emotions. He was unsettled by the ancestor's judgment and burdened by the counsel they had provided for Habe Nohi. He was not quite sure how to share the information he had received and needed some time to gather his thoughts."

"Not long at all," Habe Nohi offered, leaning forward in anticipation. "So, what did the ancestors say? Do I have their blessing to proceed with the alliance and the betrothal to seal it?"
Mai Sihiri looked at the cackling fire. His thoughts echoed deep within him like wind bouncing off the hollow walls of his cavern. *The betrothal of Amina to Sarki Ibrahim Maje would be the end of Habe Nohi?*

A spark leapt into Mai Sihiri's otherwise lackluster eyes as he recollected the words of the ancestors and an idea popped into his head. *We therefore declare that no man shall judge you but the Habe himself. If the Habe does not judge you, neither shall we or any other man judge you.*

Mai Sihiri realized that if Habe Nohi chose to proceed with the betrothal, that would be his end...and that would mean that he, Mai Sihiri, would be spared Habe Nohi's judgment.

He wondered whether what he contemplated flouted any of the ancestors' commands. He could not afford to incur additional wrath. *This is our word where that is concerned: the alliance with Katsina is good and will serve Zazzau well. But his intention to betroth Amina to Sarki Ibrahim Maje is bad. If he proceeds down that path, it will be the end of him.*

Although the ancestors had revealed the knowledge Habe Nohi sought, they had not indicated what precisely was to be shared with him or when anything was to be shared.

In the absence of explicit direction, Mai Sihiri exercised discretion in delivering ancestral counsel to any village petitioner. What he was considering right now was no different, he cogitated.

"Mai Sihiri, Mai Sihiri..."

Habe Nohi's persistent calling reached Mai Sihiri from what seemed like a distant place. By the time Mai Sihiri looked away from the fire and into the now visibly agitated eyes of Habe

Nohi, he was no longer fearful of the dire consequences associated with the information he possessed.

"Our Zazzau ancestors are jubilant for the season ahead my esteemed Habe. Now, hear me well. Our ancestors have revealed to me that the visit to Katsina will be an important milestone in Amina's destiny and for the future of Zazzau. Our ancestors are excited for the accord with Katsina as it will be a foundation stone towards a great Hausaland empire."

Mai Sihiri paused to observe Habe Nohi's reaction. He saw the Habe's features light up.

"Really? This is wonderful news, Mai Sihiri!" Habe Nohi exclaimed, raising his hands and looking upwards. "Our ancestors be praised."

"Indeed, my esteemed Habe. This is in line with our ancestors' will. Princess Amina has a great destiny. What will occur is simply a manifestation of a path prepared by our ancestors. What our ancestors require of you is that you nurture her spirit so that she may become who she is destined to be."

Habe Nohi blinked, his expression puzzled.

"Mai Sihiri, I am so very grateful to our ancestors for this news and that you always submit yourself to be their oracle of wisdom. But how am I to nurture such a destiny if I do not know or understand what she is meant to become?

She is a girl that will mature into a beautiful young woman and as our ancestors have protected her virtue, she will someday be a graceful wife and queen. But what is this destiny you speak of? Pray tell me if the ancestors have revealed more to you."

Mai Sihiri's reply was quick.

"Do as your heart guides you, my esteemed Habe. I am confident that the ancestors have a plan for Princess Amina."

Habe Nohi nodded, excited. "Now that I know my plan is blessed by the ancestors, I must move quickly to secure the alliance and fortify Zazzau as soon as possible."

He paused, his brow creased in thought.

"I need to inform my daughter and Nikitau. But, perhaps better to leave that until I return from Katsina with a favorable disposition from Sarki Ibrahim Maje."

"Mai Sihiri, I have one more question for the ancestors. I am hopeful that they will provide some suitable answer as it would ease my troubled soul."

Habe Nohi paused to see that he still had Mai Sihiri's full attention. Then, he proceeded.

"As you know, Mai Sihiri, I have no male heir and it does not appear Princess Bakwa will have any more children since it has now been sixteen seasons since she gave birth to Amina.

Is it possible that Amina will quickly conceive a male heir from her marriage to Sarki Ibrahim Maje? I am concerned about the furtherance of strong leadership and protection for the people of Zazzau when the time comes for me to join our ancestors."

Mai Sihiri observed Habe Nohi. Mai Sihiri had not considered this possibility at all, but it pleased him to think that an affirmation would further Habe Nohi's resolve to execute the marriage as quickly as possible.

"Our ancestors have spoken, my esteemed Habe Nohi. Heed their counsel and it is possible that what you say will come to pass. Your granddaughter is highly favored."

Habe Nohi's eyes lit up like stars in the night Zazzau sky. He spoke excitedly.

"Our ancestors be praised! This is wonderful news Mai Sihiri. As always you will be greatly rewarded for your service to me!"

Mai Sihiri smiled. "I live only to serve you and our ancestors, my esteemed Habe. I am exceedingly happy the ancestors have chosen to favor you and your lineage."

As Habe Nohi prepared to depart, he sounded a note of caution.

"Mai Sihiri. Please consider these discussions highly confidential until I give permission to disclose. Amina's marriage to Sarki Ibrahim Maje is an important foundation for a united Hausaland. It is therefore critical that we safeguard these plans, even from Amina herself. Knowing my free-spirited granddaughter, she will oppose the betrothal and truncate these plans if disclosed prematurely."

Mai Sihiri bowed low and swore himself to silence.

CHAPTER TWELVE

An Unexpected Turn of Events

Impossible is merely a symptom of a shackled mind

"IS MAHMUD COMING ALONG with his father today, or has he tired of you?" Amina teased Jamila. They were sitting together outside Jamila's mother's hut. It was about midday. The sun hung high in the sky, at its full might.

Jamila threw Amina a disgusted look as she wiped sweat from her forehead with the hem of her wrapper. She was hunched over a basin of spinach stems, plucking its leaves to be used in preparation of a favorite meal: tuwo shinkafa da miya kuka. The meal was being readied for Mallam Sule - Mahmud's father, who was to visit later.

"Why should I care? He couldn't keep his eyes off you last time he met you here. And you encouraged him, smiling and batting your eyelids at him. That wasn't a good look for a decent girl, much less a princess," Jamila snapped.

Amina recoiled at the sting in Jamila's words. She lost her humor.

"Okay, so he likes me. Why is that something to be ashamed of? Clearly, he likes you too or he wouldn't accompany his father to your home as often as he does. You are taking this too personally." Jamila was too hurt to stop. She piled on.

"Yes, I guess he likes me too, so I should be grateful for that. You do realize as princess, you will most certainly be betrothed to someone powerful. I am certain your betrothed will be an ugly, much older man from a village we seek to ally with."

Amina flinched. She was more upset by Jamila's spitefulness than the words she had spoken.

"Why are you being so mean?" Amina asked.

Jamila did not reply. Instead, she hissed and refocused on her spinach plucking, mumbling under her breath how Mahmud was stupid for even thinking he might have a chance with Amina.

"You know I can hear everything you are saying," Amina said.

"I suppose you can, unless your infatuation with Mahmud has made you deaf."

Amina was fed up. She rose angrily.

"I will give you time to get over yourself Jamila."

As Amina walked away, Jamila, with tears welling up in her eyes, yelled.

"You need to get over yourself, not me. You can at least acknowledge that you toyed with Mahmud even though you could see he liked me."

Amina walked briskly. She realized Jamila spoke truth about her behavior towards Mahmud. But she did not feel the need to apologize for the boy's admiration. His admiration made her feel powerful, and she would do it again without pause.

Amina felt offended and worried at Jamila's spiteful suggestion that she would be betrothed. She realized how probable it was given her status as princess. But she reassured herself that grandfather Nohi would never sanction a betrothal if it meant hurting her.

Amina soon found herself walking along a major pathway on her way home. This pathway demarcated the southeast wall of the palace courtyard from the village dwellings. She kicked angrily at small rocks on the ground as she tried to suppress thoughts of ever being betrothed to an ugly, older man.

As she walked, she tried to redirect her thoughts. She glanced in the opposite direction of the palace courtyard wall to her left, wishing she knew where Mahmud lived. Her heartbeat quickened as she considered going in search of him to spite Jamila.

But it was not merely the idea of spiting Jamila that excited her. She imagined that she had enchanted Mahmud and longed to experience power over him again. A small smile crossed her lips. Amina was developing a plan to go in search of Mahmud when she noticed Aisha, her maidservant, running like the wind in her direction and yelling some unintelligible words.

Behind Aisha, two armed guards followed with equal haste. Alarmed that there was some danger, Amina began sprinting towards her as well. As she closed in on Aisha, Amina heard what she was saying.

"Princess Amina, I must fetch the royal midwife, Princess Bakwa is ill!"

Amina's heart sank. Her mother had shown no sign of illness when she left home earlier that day.

Perhaps Baba has hurt Mama in some way.

She panicked. Her lips tightened. Her blood boiled.

She hesitated, trying to decide what to do. She yearned to go comfort her mother, and possibly challenge her father. But fetching the royal midwife was most critical at this point.

Amina grabbed Aisha by the arms, shaking her hard as though attempting to shake the truth out of her.

"What happened? What is the matter with my mother?"

"I don't know." Aisha said, out of breath. "All I know is I was told to fetch the royal midwife as Princess Bakwa has taken ill."

Amina bolted in the direction of the village corridors dragging Aisha by one arm. "Together, we can find her quickly. We must find her quickly."

Soon the royal midwife was contacted, and the group hurried back to the palace.

A weary Princess Bakwa was seated on the floor in her hut, loosely clothed in a thin nighttime wrapper. Behind her, two royal guards fanned her with large fans made from huge raffia leaves. Two maidservants stood at a distance, ready to serve if called upon.

Another pair of maidservants stood much closer to the princess. One held a basin into which Princess Bakwa retched. The other comforted her by continuously rubbing her back in a gentle soothing fashion.

Amina stood close to the hut doorway, observing her mother with a stricken look. There was no evidence to suggest that her father had hurt her mother. Although somewhat relieved by this, Amina could not relax.

If her father was blameless then what or who was to blame? Nikitau, stood a few feet away from Amina observing Princess Bakwa with a face contoured with concern as well.

Amina glared at her father. *I am sure he is not really concerned for Mama. His concern is for his position,* she thought. If anything happens to Mama, his position in the royal family and as a member of Habe Nohi's noble council men, would be in jeopardy.

Inside the hut, the royal midwife - an elderly, gray haired woman with energy akin to a woman half her age, had requested that Princess Bakwa be transferred to her mud-brick bed for comfort. The midwife now busied herself examining her.

"Is she going to be all right?" Amina asked.

"I will know what ails her soon, your highness," the midwife replied to Amina with her back still turned to everyone.

She furrowed her brow, her hands carefully but expertly probing Princess Bakwa's temples, her head, shoulders, and belly.

Princess Bakwa looked upon the midwife with great anticipation in her eyes. Finally, the midwife was satisfied with her assessment. She ceased her examination, turned to Nikitau and the rest of the observants, and flashed a wide, dirty-toothed smile.

"Let me be the first to congratulate you *mai gida, mai karifi*. Your wife, Princess Bakwa, is with child."

The midwife's words were initially met with stunned silence. Incredulous faces spoke louder than words.

With child? After sixteen seasons?

Princess Bakwa shouted for joy, slicing through the cloud of disbelief that had descended on the hut.

Amina, bursting with euphoria, rushed to her exuberant mother's side.

"Mama, you are pregnant? I'm going to have a sibling? Our ancestors be praised."

The maidservants and guards in the room began whispering excitedly. This was wonderful news for the village. There was a chance a Prince could be born. Habe Nohi would be pleased.

Nikitau cracked a wry smile. "Our ancestors be praised indeed," he said, his voice barely audible.

He walked over to his wife and kissed her lightly on the forehead. Then, he placed a hand affectionately on Amina's cheek, spared her a half smile, and exited the hut.

Amina wasn't surprised by her father's subdued reaction, but she didn't care to ponder his action. Celebrations had already begun in the hut, and Princess Bakwa ordered that the news be delivered to her father at once.

The celebrations spread across the village as soon as Habe Nohi was informed. He immediately showered his pregnant daughter with gifts of gold jewelry and expensive indigo dyed wrappers.

He ordered a three-day palace courtyard celebration with a nightly bonfire feast. Fat cows, rotund-bellied goats, and plump chickens were rushed to the slaughter area as the royal cooks prepared a feast for the village. The entire village was soon engulfed in a frenzy of activity and excitement that peaked in a tidal wave of nighttime celebrations.

That night, Amina gathered with thousands of Zazzau villagers at the open palace courtyard, gleefully honoring the Habe's invitation to party.

The villagers were treated to palace entertainment around a crackling sky-high bonfire that lit up the night with dazzling sparks. A troupe of female dancers danced before the Habe and members of the royal household at a far end of the courtyard.

The dancers were dressed in small wrappers tied around their breasts and waists. Their faces and shoulders were painted in white, symbolic of a baby's innocence and purity. The remainder of their bodies were covered in extravagant cowrie shell bands and bracelets.

The dancers twirled to the musical beats emanating from an assembly of drummers. Standing next to the drummers, palace trumpeters periodically played the *Kakaki* - long metal trumpets reserved for royal traditional festivities.

Amina sat in a corner of the palace courtyard away from most of the crowd. She was savoring a tasty meal of peppered, roasted goat meat on the bone and roasted corn on the cob when Jamila appeared from around a corner.

She walked up to Amina.

Amina threw her a dirty look and turned away, dropping a corn cob she had been digging into.

"*Haba.* Don't be that way Amina. You know I didn't mean what I said the other day," Jamila said. She folded her arms. Her eyes and voice conveyed her apology despite her defensive posture.

Amina's eyes flashed. "You didn't mean to suggest that I should be enslaved into marriage with an ugly, older man who would maltreat me perhaps even worse than my father does my mother?"

"*Haba, ba baka ba.* How long have we been friends? You know in my heart I mean you no harm at all. I was upset but I did not mean what I said." Jamila slid beside her and nudged her playfully.

Amina was still angry that Jamila had even suggested such a thing. But she realized her friend was right. Their bond was stronger than an argument over a boy.

Amina stole a glance at Jamila who was looking up at her with longing eyes seeking forgiveness.

Amina laughed.

"Ok, maybe I will forgive you this one time. But just this..."

Amina had not finished speaking when a familiar voice cut in.

"Hello Princess Amina."

It was Mahmud standing before them. He broke into a smile with eyes only for Amina.

The girls had been so engrossed in their conversation, they failed to notice him approach.

Amina froze. Her heartbeat quickened. Kai, she thought. *Why did he have to show up now?*

She hesitated, then stole another glance at Jamila.

Jamila looked despondently from Mahmud to Amina. She locked eyes with Amina and her eyes flooded with tears. She looked back at Mahmud. Amina followed her eyes and blinked coyly. Mahmud was still fixated on her like a moth to light. Jamila was not even present, not to him.

"How are you princess?" Mahmud ventured further, his voice cracking, halting his speech.

He cleared his throat and tried again, a sheepish smile still plastered on his face like a tightly fastened mask.

"I was hoping the openness of the festivities for your mother would provide an opportunity to meet you again. And here we are."

Jamila hissed and lash out. "Go away Mahmud. Why are you disturbing us?"

Amina threw Jamila a reprimanding look. She felt trapped between her desire for Mahmud's attention and guilt for her friend's unhappiness. She decided to try a gentler, friendlier tone in cognizance of her friend's feelings.

Amina nudged Jamila. "Don't be like that, Jamila. Mahmud is merely saying hello." She flashed Mahmud a sweet smile. Mahmud's satisfied smile grew so wide, the corners of his lips almost touched his ears.

Jamila threw Amina the look of death. Amina avoided her friend's dagger eyes. She knew what she was doing but didn't want to stop. *Why can't Jamila just accept the situation?*

"Amina, *menene wannan*? Why are you doing this?" Jamila asked. She choked back tears. But they spilled onto her cheeks. She began to whimper.

Amina was torn. She reached out to comfort Jamila.

Mahmud, like a man released from a trance, seemed to notice Jamila for the first time and reached out to comfort her as well.

"Leave me alone," Jamila snapped, slapping their hands away. "You two deserve each other!"

She rose abruptly and ran off, sobbing.

Amina and Mahmud remained silent in the immediate aftermath of Jamila's departure. Mahmud kept his eyes on Jamila's retreating figure until it disappeared into the celebrating crowd. Amina kept her eyes on Mahmud. She felt bad for Jamila but presumed they would reconcile again when the time was right.

Amina was keen to explore Mahmud's intentions, and to enjoy the strange power that she had over him. The fact that Mahmud appeared unperturbed by traditional norms, which forbade a male commoner from showing such interest in a princess, heightened her excitement. She stifled all cautionary thoughts.

Amina finally rose and grabbed Mahmud by the wrist when it seemed he would never stop staring after Jamila.

"Don't worry," Amina said in the softest voice she could muster. "Jamila is my friend. I know she will get over it."

Mahmud nodded, recovering his plastered smile while allowing Amina to guide him to sit next to her where Jamila had sat.

CHAPTER THIRTEEN

A Secret Plot

One who trusts a mischief maker is like he who takes a net to draw water from a well

THE SOUTH END OF Zazzau, far away from the festive palace courtyard, remained eerily quiet like a place frozen out of the current celebratory time. Here, the dark and quiet of night suffused the atmosphere like a somber cloud, uninterrupted by the bonfire light, the joyful music, or the village laughter.

Shrouded by the dark, a man wrapped in a cloak, hurried towards Zazzau's prison pit situated near the foot of the hills at Zazzau's rear.

The prison pit was twenty-foot deep – wide enough to fit many prisoners at once. It was sealed and secured at the top with huge metal chains.

Close to the pit was a small hut where the prison pit keeper dwelled. At present, the pit was packed with Zazzau's most notorious offenders, one of whom was of interest to the cloaked man that approached in the dark.

The cloaked man arrived at the hut and announced his arrival in hushed tones while looking around to ensure he was not followed.

The prison pit keeper - a big burly man, quickly let the man into the hut.

"Mutuwa Dole, what can I do for you or your master this time?"

Mutuwa Dole reached into a side knot of his large wrapper and unknotted cowries shells which he carefully handed to the prison pit keeper. The cowrie shells appeared to gleam from the reflection cast by a flame dancing on an oil wick.

"Mai Yari," Mutuwa Dole began, addressing the pit keeper by name and handing the cowrie shells to him. "My master thanks you as always for your service and has authorized me to give you fifty cowrie shells in exchange for a favor."

The guard beamed with pleasure as the white façade of the shells came into view and he accepted them.

"Mutuwa Dole, what is it your master requires this time? When will you reveal your master's identity? Have I not earned his trust yet?"

Mutuwa Dole scowled. "No! My master's identity must remain hidden. Do not dare dabble into matters that do not concern you. In due course, all who have assisted my master will be fully rewarded.

My master has a connection to great wealth. Therefore, be comforted in the fact that you, my friend, are on his list of those to be rewarded when the time is right. But do not pry further. Simply ensure that all actions you undertake on his behalf remain secret. If you do, you will remain in his favor."

Mai Yari apologized for his curiosity.

"You have a prisoner in your prison pit with no family or next of kin," Mutuwa Dole continued. "His name is Mustapha. He awaits the Habe's judgment for attempting to rape a girl called Aisha who is now a maidservant in the royal palace. Do you know the prisoner of whom I speak?"

"Yes, of course," Mai Yari replied.

"Excellent. My master requires his head!"

Mai Yari did not flinch at the request. This pleased Mutuwa Dole. He continued.

"His execution is destined to serve a greater purpose and his head is required for this purpose. I assume this task carries minimal risk to you personally given Mustapha is of no consequence to anyone in the village.

You are to report to the Habe that he attempted to kill some of the other prisoners in the pit and ended up a victim of his own foolishness. It will be noted that Mustapha died as he lived, a fool with no kin. Is that clear?"

Mai Yari stared at the cowrie shells he had been given. Then, he looked at Mutuwa Dole with searching eyes.

"Mutuwa Dole. The master's work is always dirty. In the past, he has required me to rough someone up or threaten someone. But this one is a greater request. Normally, I would hesitate to kill any of the Habe's prisoners. But, in the case of Mustapha, you are correct. I don't think anyone will miss a such a random prisoner. But..." Mai Yari paused and looked down at the cowrie shells again.

Mutuwa Dole read Mai Yari's mind.

"You want more because this is a killing."

Mai Yari smiled. His teeth were colored red from excessive kola nut chewing.

"*Kai*, Mutuwa Dole. "You are a mind reader, *fa. Walahi*, your master is so wise for appointing a smart man like you to handle his business."

Mutuwa Dole sneered. This wasn't the first time Mai Yari had asked for more than he was offered. In fact, he always found a reason to ask for more. But his service was needed. He had to be tolerated and compensated until such a time when he could be discarded.

"You will get more when the deed is done. Okay?"
Mai Yari was quiet, his eyes still on the cowries, apparently considering.

"Am I to wait forever for a reply?"

Mai Yari laughed awkwardly. "*Madallah*! Very good. We have an accord. Your master's instructions are clear."

Mutuwa Dole smiled, pleased his task had been accomplished.

"Very good Mai Yari. I will return tomorrow about this time to collect Mustapha's head."

CHAPTER FOURTEEN

The Katsina Alliance – Sarki Ibrahim Maje

In a negotiation, he who seeks a fair deal above all else ends up with nothing, or worse

IT WAS A SUNNY afternoon under a cloudless sky in the village of Katsina, about three days horseback journey, north of Zazzau. Thousands of Katsina citizens were gathered in the dusty plain of Ambuttai, the meeting place for all important matters of the village, situated next to the palace grounds of Katsina's ruler.

The excitement amongst the crowd was palpable as the citizens awaited the emergence of their ruler, Sarki Ibrahim Maje, who had summoned them to share some important news.

The boisterous crowd was gathered at the foot of Gobarau Minaret, a massive tower built with mudbricks and clay. This tower, constructed over several generations, was a monument of immense pride for the people of Katsina and provided a grand, elevated platform from which their ruler often made important announcements and proclamations.

Sarki Ibrahim Maje readied himself to appear before his people. He was waiting in an enclosure carved at the tower's summit. His royal announcer, a young male servant, was addressing the expectant crowd below. He was reminding them of the many accomplishments of their ruler while also lavishing customary platitudes on him.

As the royal announcer excelled in lyrical praise and exultation of his ruler, Sarki Ibrahim Maje's mind drifted to a place far away from his kingdom, a place he had recently visited.

He reminisced of the experiences that had led him to this moment. He had journeyed to visit the Askia of the Songhai empire, west of Hausaland. There, he visited the capital city, Gao, and its famed commercial city, Timbuktu.

Sarki Ibrahim Maje had been amazed at the significant number of academic scholars he encountered – scholars educated in astronomy, sciences, and, Arabic writing.

Although he was already familiar with Timbuktu's reputation as a trading port, the expansive degree of complex commerce emanating from the beautiful city astonished him.

Caravans trading in salt, kola nuts, cowries, and natural resources such as gold, copper, and iron traversed bustling routes almost nonstop from Timbuktu, Gao, and the north African Maghreb world to the smaller cities of Niani and Begho to the south.

Sarki Ibrahim Maje had journeyed to Gao to seek an alliance with the powerful Emperor Askia Daud, whose Songhai empire dominated more than a third of the entire west African region.

Askia Daud was the grandson of Askia – "The Great Visionary" – who expanded the Songhai empire east from Gao to the heart of West Africa, south to the Atlantic coast, and far north to the outskirts of the Sahara Desert.

Under the Askias, the Songhai empire had progressed so much that it now controlled all trans-Saharan trade routes eastward to the Egyptian city of Cairo and northward across the Sahara, reaching the Maghreb city of Tunis.

Sarki Ibrahim Maje had asked the mighty emperor for tributary control of the trans Saharan trade route that passed through Katsina, onto Kano and beyond to Cairo. In return, and as a gesture of loyalty, Sarki Ibrahim Maje converted to Islam and pledged Katsina as an Islamic state.

Sarki Ibrahim Maje was recalled from his reverie by the familiar culmination of the customary oration. It was time to appear before the people.

He emerged from his enclosure at the tower's summit, welcomed by thunderous applause and cheers from his fervent followers below. The Sarki was a short, bald headed man with a rotund body. His numerous guards, in stark contrast, were bare-chested monuments of manliness.

Sarki Ibrahim Maje waved slowly to the thronging crowd and walked to his throne – a clay throne decorated with stringed golden orbs and two long elephant tusks jutting out of both arm rests. He was adorned in a long, purple cotton robe and a white turban gifted to him by Askia Daud during his recent trip.

As Sarki Ibrahim Maje surveyed the vast crowd before him, waiting for the applause and wild cheering to wane, his eyes beamed with excitement about the vision he intended to share with his people.

"My people," Sarki Ibrahim Maje began. He spoke haltingly, picking his words for emphasis and to ensure his voice carried far and wide across his audience. Each word he spoke echoed, adding an impressive aura and pomp to his rendition.

"As you know, I have recently returned from my sojourn to the wondrous cities of the Songhai empire. I must tell you all that the stories we have heard of Songhai pale in comparison to the grandeur I witnessed firsthand."

He paused for an extended period to allow this declaration register, while running his eyes across the length and breadth of the faces looking up at him with enthusiasm. It was so quiet amongst the attentive crowd that one could hear a nail drop.

Sarki Ibrahim Maje continued. "I must confess that I was well inspired by the grandeur of which I speak. I was motivated and excited. Therefore, I have returned to you, determined to do everything in my power to establish such grandeur right here in our beautiful Katsina."

The crowd erupted in wild cheers and applause once more.

When the cheers ceased, Sarki Ibrahim Maje continued. "In the magnificent cities of Gao and Timbuktu, I saw prosperity and knowledge flow abundantly like the waters of the great River Niger.

Dwellings in these cities shimmer all day long as the sun's rays dance on their gold-plated city walls. In these cities, there are high places of learning filled with wondrous artifacts of science, astronomy, and all manner of knowledge.

Traders from regions far and wide, seeking favor with Songhai, eagerly grant significant trade concessions that greatly benefit the Askia dynasty. And Emperor Askia Daud, being the great leader that he is, prospers all Songhai subjects accordingly. Therefore, in these cities, even men and women of no authority and limited means dress radiantly in silk and cotton.

In these cities, jewelry abounds plentiful like the sand in our village pathways. In these cities, food is plentiful beyond belief. They have salt and fish, kola nuts and pepper, yam and oil. Whatever you can imagine, they have it all in abundance. I quickly concluded that to be a subject of Songhai means to lack nothing at all.

When I asked the eminent emperor how it was that Songhai had become so great, he replied as follows, 'It is the grace of almighty Allah. All who worship Allah can expect to someday prosper as such and even attain greater heights of prosperity should they desire. Allah is merciful and benevolent, and he provides for all who seek him with total commitment.'"

Sarki Ibrahim Maje paused again before stretching out his left hand towards the royal announcer. On cue, the announcer placed a large metal sword in his hand.

This sword was the *Gajere*, the royal sword by which the law was pronounced and sealed by the Sarki of Katsina. It was believed to have been used by the legendary founder of Katsina, Korau, to win freedom from the Durbawa dynasty many generations before.

Sarki Ibrahim Maje grasped the sword handle with both hands as firmly as he could. He raised it high and stepped forward with the pointed edge facing the sky. He moved as close to the edge of the elevated enclosure as he could.

"My people, it is only an ostrich that keeps its head buried in the sand when there is an abundant supply of food nearby. We, the people of Katsina, will not act like the ostrich. I have discovered a path to prosperity for our village and determined that we must take advantage of it.

Therefore, to you this day, I make the same pledge I made to his eminence; Emperor Askia Daud. I declare my loyalty to Allah the one true God and to his favored servant Askia Daud of Songhai.

I decree that all Katsina citizens must serve Allah so that he might prosper us and defend us like he has done to the Askias of Songhai. As a symbol of faithfulness, I declare that I, with the help of Emperor Askia Daud, will build a magnificent mosque on this ground. This mosque shall be a wonder to all of Hausaland; a befitting place of worship to almighty Allah."

There was silence for a while. Then applause began below. It was slow at first but soon swelled to a thunderous crescendo. Satisfied with the reception from his people, Sarki Ibrahim Maje smiled and stepped back, handing the sword back to the royal announcer.

The transport by which he had ascended the tower had been readied for his descent – a wooden carriage harnessed by six sturdy ropes fashioned from thick leather. This wooden carriage was operated by a massive metallic pulley built on the ground below.

Sarki Ibrahim Maje's guards grabbed and steadied the carriage at the mouth of the tower's summit. When they had gained enough control of it, they motioned to the Sarki who proceeded to board the carriage as carefully as he could.

Once he was comfortably seated on one of two small wooden benches chained to the wooden floor inside the carriage, the guards motioned to the two pulley operators down below. The operators, their oiled muscles heaving and gleaming in the sunlight, began to lower the wooden carriage to the ground below.

Sarki Ibrahim Maje's palace was only a stone throw from the tower. He entered his palace compound flanked by his guards and preceded by a small entourage of royal servants who always accompanied him wherever he went to ensure his every whim was duly attended to.

As soon as his entourage set foot on palace grounds, a royal announcer sounded a trumpet and bellowed loudly.

"*Ranka ya Dade* Sarki Ibrahim Maje, *Sannu da zuwa mai karifi.*"

The front end of the palace compound, closer to the palatial huts, was filled with benches typically occupied by village folk who came seeking wisdom and counsel from their ruler. At this moment, however, the benches were empty except for a group of about fifteen people whom Sarki Ibrahim Maje instantly observed to be foreigners.

These foreigners had arisen upon arrival of the Sarki and his entourage and now remained standing as the Sarki walked past them before ascending the few stone steps to his bronze throne. Once the Sarki was seated on his throne, all members of his entourage seated themselves in a circle on the bare floor around his throne and the guards took up positions on either side of the throne.

Sarki Ibrahim Maje's advisory council of noble men filed out from an inner palace chamber and slowly took their seats on two elongated wooden benches adjacent to the throne. These nobles were more than just an advisory council to the Sarki. They served as his spiritual protection as well – covered in charms and amulets specially conjured by the village sorcerer for the Sarki's protection.

Once Sarki Ibrahim Maje was settled onto his throne, he scrutinized his guests and broke into a warm smile of recognition. His guests were Habe Nohi and esteemed delegates from Zazzau.

Sarki Ibrahim Maje had been informed of their intended visit and purpose by a Zazzau forerunner sent many days earlier. Eagerly, Sarki Ibrahim Maje scanned the delegates for his proposed bride, anxious to see if she was worthy of the lavish words of beauty the Zazzau forerunner had ascribed to her.

He did not have to look far for his eyes instantly fell upon a young woman standing by the Habe, observing the expansive palace compound. He licked his lips, permitting his eyes to linger on her stunning beauty.

The young woman before him was strikingly tall, just like her grandfather. Her skin seemed smooth as burnished bronze and her clear, wide eyes shone bright like polished cowrie shells displayed on dark wood.

This beautiful woman had high cheekbones and a long thin face, as though her face were sculpted. Her lips were full and invitingly supple. She was dressed in a flowing purple dress and matching head turban with a striking red ruby at its center.

The head turban was wrapped around her forehead leaving the top of her head exposed to reveal her strands of her dark hair stylishly braided. The braids cascaded in elongated strands down her face, culminating in blue beads just above her neck.

Only when her roaming eyes finally found and held his, did the Sarki realize he had lost himself in her beauty. He locked his excited eyes with hers, trying to establish a claim over the paragon that was soon to be promised to him.

Sarki Ibrahim Maje held her eyes until she looked away, then he smiled. He was pleased to observe what he interpreted as the nervous, submissive reaction of the beautiful young woman that was to be his bride.

The royal announcer who announced the Sarki's arrival at the palace now stood beside his ruler and made his second pronouncement of the day.

"Your royal highness, esteemed Sarki Ibrahim Maje, I hereby announce the presence of his royal highness Habe Nohi of Zazzau, accompanied by his esteemed delegates."

As the announcer said these words, he motioned to the group of foreigners gathered in the courtyard. Habe Nohi stepped forward from the delegates along with his two trusted guards and Amina.

Sarki Ibrahim Maje and his council of nobles rose respectfully in traditional welcoming of their esteemed guests. He stepped down from his throne and advanced towards Habe Nohi, who walked towards the Sarki as well.

When the two Hausa leaders met, each ruler raised his right arm and gently struck the other's forearm three times in quick succession nodding in customary, royal salutation each time. Then each raised the left arm and repeated the customary royal gesture.

"*Sannu da Zuwa* Habe Nohi. It is a high honor to have you visit us in Katsina land. I am delighted to welcome you. I apologize that I kept you waiting. I had some very important village matters to attend to."

Habe Nohi returned his host's greeting with similar enthusiasm and acknowledged that he and his delegates were honored to be guests in Katsina.

Sarki Ibrahim Maje smiled and clasped his palms in a single, loud clap.

"Rest, food, and drink for our esteemed guests. Tonight, after you have rested, Habe Nohi, we shall discuss the undoubtedly noble purpose of your visit."

At the sound of the Sarki's clap, several servants emerged from the palatial huts behind the gathering and began to dutifully attend to Habe Nohi's delegates.

Habe Nohi nodded to his opposite ruler in appreciation of the hospitality. But Sarki Ibrahim Maje's attention was already captured elsewhere. Habe Nohi followed the Sarki's eyes and smiled when he discovered that the Sarki was staring at Amina. She seemed to be doing her best to avoid his probing eyes.

Sarki Ibrahim Maje was delighted that Amina appeared to naturally exude what he perceived to be a seductive, coquettish aura – a powerful charm for any young woman who would captivate a suitor.

She will make a fine second wife, he thought to himself.

CHAPTER FIFTEEN

The Katsina Alliance – Habe Nohi

Negotiation is like a fierce battle. To engage otherwise is to lose

THAT EVENING, DINNER WAS served in a personal, intimate setting in Sarki Ibrahim Maje's private dinner chamber. Habe Nohi and Amina sat on a mat opposite from Sarki Ibrahim Maje and his wife, Queen Zainab.

Habe Nohi scanned the chamber. Along the inside perimeter, oil wicks burned dimly on tall stilts. Beside each stilt, a muscular, bare-chested guard stood still like a stone statue. The chamber was carved out of the smallest of five conjoined huts that together formed the inner palace of the royal Katsina family.

The mats upon which the diners sat were spread on the bare floor but cushioned with soft cotton underneath to provide comfort. Before each mat was a table spread with a feast of food.

There was an assortment of delicious mangoes, oranges, and bananas. There were freshly boiled yams with freshly prepared pepper stew. There were kola nuts and alligator pepper aplenty. And there was juicy antelope meat, which had been skewered and roasted over a slow burning fire. There was plenty to drink as well – fermented Burukutu, water, and fresh milk.

When the royal families had eaten to their heart's content and exchanged pleasantries about the weather and state of affairs in their various lands, Habe Nohi began to speak of the purpose for which he had come.

"Esteemed Sarki Ibrahim Maje. Our people say an urgent matter on the mind is like waste in the bowel. It must never be delayed longer than is necessary. So, it is time for us to discuss the purpose of my visit; a matter of utmost urgency for both our villages and indeed for all of Hausaland."

Once Queen Zainab heard Habe Nohi utter these words, she signaled to Amina that it was time for them to leave the two rulers to discuss the important matter at hand.

"Come, my dear Princess Amina, let me show you around the rest of our palace and dwellings."

Amina frowned and hesitated. But when she caught her father's eyes signaling that she should follow Queen Zainab's lead, she rose and exited the room hand-in-hand with the queen.

Habe Nohi watched Sarki Ibrahim Maje's eyes follow the pair as they exited the hut. He was happy to see that the Sarki's eyes narrowed in on his granddaughter's figure. Habe Nohi cleared his throat to get the Sarki's attention.

"Sarki Ibrahim Maje, my sources tell me that Etsu Tsudi of Nupeland is gaining in strength and readying a mighty army to attack Hausaland. The ambitious pig is determined to infiltrate and seize our lands, murder our men, rape our women, and enslave our children.

My scouts tell me that he considers conquest of Hausaland a necessity to gain free trade passage to the illustrious city of Cairo and the lands beyond that stretch to Baghdad.

Furthermore, I have learned that, despite his prior defeat, he intends to once again target my beloved Zazzau as his entry point to Hausaland given we are closest to Nupe.

Next time he attacks, he will likely have all clans of the Nupe confederacy aligned with him. Should he succeed, I have no doubt that he will make his way further north to Katsina and Kano."

Habe Nohi paused, rubbing his beard.

Sarki Ibrahim Maje held his guest's gaze, then looked down at his mat, nodding as he appeared to consider what he had just heard. He shut his eyes and clasped his palms together, deep in thought. He did not remain silent much longer.

"I agree with you, Habe Nohi, that the pig called Etsu Tsudi, should never be allowed an incursion into Hausaland. I was informed by your forerunner who journeyed here a few days ago, that you are offering your beautiful granddaughter's hand to me in marriage to seal a proposed alliance. Is this true?"

Habe Nohi laughed loudly and rubbed his hands together like a player who had just secured an advantage over his opponent. "So, you like Amina, eh? Tell me, is she not stunningly beautiful and to be desired by all men?"

Sarki Ibrahim Maje now laughed loudly in return.

"Well, Princess Amina is maturing into a wonderful young woman and I must agree that she is indeed exceedingly beautiful and absolutely desirable. In fact, she has stolen my mind already. A union with her is befitting and it shall be the seal of alliance between our two villages. However, there is one additional consideration or condition."

Sarki Ibrahim Maje paused and leaned closer to his guest. Habe Nohi, pleased by the words he had heard the Sarki speak thus far, now raised his eyebrows in question. He had expected something like this, given Sarki Ibrahim Maje's reputation for tough negotiations. What could the additional consideration be?

The Sarki continued, seeing he had his guest's attention. "I must inform you that the value of your alliance with Katsina has been enhanced by an alliance I recently secured with Emperor Askia Daud of Songhai."

Habe Nohi eyes widened in excited disbelief. "Fada gaskiya Sarki Ibrahim Maje?"

"*Walahi!*" Sarki Ibrahim Maje replied.

"This is excellent news Sarki Ibrahim Maje. With the full backing of the Songhai empire, Etsu Tsudi does not stand a chance against us no matter how many Nupe clans he succeeds in adding to his ranks."

Sarki Ibrahim Maje nodded. "Yes, indeed Habe Nohi. I am pleased that you yourself see how much more valuable your proposed alliance with Katsina is now.

Therefore, although Princess Amina is undoubtedly a dream bride, duty demands that I request an enhanced offer from you. This will ensure that any alliance between Zazzau and Katsina is securely bonded in a truly honorable and fair manner."

Habe Nohi gathered his flowing babban rigga about him in thought. He grinned at his host's unsurprising tactful negotiation. Sarki Ibrahim Maje had a reputation for being cunning.

Habe Nohi had anticipated something like this to occur and had been prepared to offer gifts of livestock and natural resources in addition to Amina's hand in marriage.

But given this new information, Habe Nohi sensed that the additional gifts he would be required to offer might be insufficient. Given Sarki Ibrahim Maje's alliance with Songhai, Habe Nohi now desperately desired an alliance with Katsina. The Sarki was clearly playing a winning hand.

"Very well Sarki. What is it you desire in addition to my precious granddaughter's hand in marriage?"

"Ten thousand pounds of gold!"

Habe Nohi recoiled like one struck hard across the face.

"*Haba* Sarki. It is a fool's errand to draw from one's well in a bid to grow a garden in a desert. Respectfully, even if I could pay such a hefty price, my treasury will be ruined thereafter. What then will an alliance mean to a village that is completely drained of its treasury?"

An awkward silence ensued after which Sarki Ibrahim Maje sighed and said. "Very well, I am a reasonable man, and I appreciate Princess Amina's beauty. She is truly most desirable. Therefore, I am willing to seal our agreement for eight thousand pounds of gold, and Princess Amina's hand in marriage. Below this price, I cannot see a deal."

Habe Nohi shook his head. He looked down at his mat. He had not foreseen this dire of a negotiation. As badly as he wanted this alliance, Zazzau could not afford to be perceived as begging for it. Zazzau was a proud village and extensive haggling would damage his village's reputation.

The backing of Songhai would be a dream for any village but at what price? Eight thousand pounds of gold would significantly upgrade Sarki Ibrahim Maje's military resources and enrich Katsina's treasury for years to come. But it would significantly deplete Zazzau's coffers.

Habe Nohi looked up at the Sarki. The Sarki was watching him with keen interest, looking like a man clearly aware of his advantage in the negotiation.

Habe Nohi struggled to conceal his anger at being cornered into this position. Sarki Ibrahim Maje should have conveyed such demands to the forerunner to allow due time for consideration. This was a crafty move by the Sarki and Habe Nohi did not appreciate such guile. But any response required civility akin to nobility.

"Alright Sarki Ibrahim Maje. You have made your conditions known. Although I remain very interested in our alliance, I must ask for some time to consider your conditions and confer with my nobles back in my village.

I am honored that you would consider Amina, my granddaughter worthy to be a queen in your land, equal to the beautiful Queen Zainab. But there are protocols that must be observed to formalize the union.

I am sure you will appreciate that I must take the exciting news that you are keen to marry Amina back to her parents. Amina herself is yet unaware of her future. Allow me to pay due attention to the fulfillment of essential protocols while I consider you counter proposal and then we shall reconvene at a future date. Is this acceptable to you?"

"Of course!" Sarki Ibrahim Maje responded. He lifted a gourd filled with Burukutu high into the air and proposed a toast. "Come, my dear Habe Nohi. Let us cast official matters aside for the moment and celebrate a unison of hearts and minds and a furtherance of our common cause."

Habe Nohi obliged, forcing a cheery demeanor. But his mind was already evaluating alternatives for future negotiations

CHAPTER SIXTEEN

The Katsina Alliance - Amina

When two Elephants fight, the ground underneath need not suffer in silence...it may choose to swallow them whole

AMINA AND QUEEN ZAINAB were relaxing in Queen Zainab's hut, adjoined to the Sarki Ibrahim Maje's hut by a tall mud wall. Through a small window in the hut, the moon cast an enchanting light upon a wide stream only a few stone throws from the Sarki's palace courtyard. Both Queen Zainab and Amina lay on straw mats, each fanned by a guard.

Amina had been reluctant to leave the Sarki and her grandfather when they were about to discuss the very matters of strategic alliance she was so keen to understand. But she had enjoyed the tour Queen Amina gave her of the seven conjoined huts and the open palace courtyard.

They had visited the palace shrine in one of the huts where the *Gajere* sword, and other battle artifacts including a spear, shield and charms believed to have been used by Korau, the legendary founder of Katsina, were displayed. The Katsina palace environ was not much different from that of Zazzau, Amina had observed.

"What is it like to be a queen?" Amina asked Queen Zainab, observing her round face in the shadow of the moonlit night. Queen Zainab had shared that she was betrothed to Sarki Ibrahim Maje by her parents from birth and was married to him as soon as she began to mature into womanhood.

Queen Zainab shrugged and adjusted her black hijab, tightening it a bit more on the side of her face to prevent it from sliding off. She was still getting used to wearing a hijab as was required of a Muslim wife.

"All my life, I have been groomed to be queen, so I don't really know any different. When you are betrothed from birth, everything you do is geared towards ensuring you are perfect for your husband. I am always at his service."

Queen Zainab caught Amina's disgusted reaction to her words and burst into laughter.

"Dear Princess, you are still young. I remember feeling like you do now not too long ago. But I quickly embraced my destiny. You know, it's not bad to be desired by one so powerful as the Sarki. Some might say it is the ultimate love potion."

Queen Zainab winked at Amina.

Amina glared at Queen Zainab for a moment. Sarki Ibrahim Maje was a short, rotund man – a stark contrast from her grandfather's stately stature which she had come to associate with rulership.

Not bad to be desired by a fat ugly ruler? The ultimate love potion?

Amina almost spat out of revulsion. She observed how roundish and plump Queen Zainab's cheeks looked. Although she was older than Amina by many seasons, Queen Zainab's face had a more childlike appearance.

I'm sure you are quite the plaything for him so long as he keeps you well fed, Amina thought.

"I can think of many other ways to feel powerful besides reducing myself to a man's plaything," Amina said, her eyes flashing in the moonlight's glare. "I do wonder how men would feel if they were made our playthings for a change."

Queen Zainab laughed again and shook her head at her young companion.

"That, my dear Princess Amina, is like imagining you wake up one day and the sun is gone from the sky. It will never happen. You should embrace your womanhood and the power therein. It seems to me that you did not notice the way my husband looked at you. He desires you."

Amina shot her a disgusted look. "What?"

Queen Zainab laughed aloud again.

"But for your clearly visible womanly attributes, I would call you a child. Clearly, you are still unaware of the ways of a man and a woman. Let me say it again. My husband desires you."

Amina blinked and squeezed her face in disgust. She had found Sarki Ibrahim Maje's lustful glare off-putting but had not considered that he might actually want to lay with her. He wouldn't dare. She was Habe Nohi's granddaughter, after all.

"And, suppose this is true. It does not trouble you?" Amina asked.

Queen Zainab shrugged. "He is my Sarki and my Lord. He is allowed more than one wife by tradition and even by our newfound Islam religion. If he desires you and asks for you to be his wife, I must not object. And I do like you. Your innocence...and stubbornness is quite refreshing."

Amina's eyes fell to the dusty earth between her and Queen Zainab. Could there be any doubt? Queen Zainab sounded so sure. What if her grandfather and Sarki Ibrahim Maje were discussing her future at this very moment? Surely grandfather would not barter away her life in such a crude manner?

"Come now," Queen Zainab said. "Don't look so sullen." She grabbed Amina by the hand and pulled her to her feet. "Marriages don't happen overnight so I wouldn't worry too much. Come, let me show you the cowrie shell necklaces our villagers presented to me during our recently concluded harvest festival."

CHAPTER SEVENTEEN

The Plot is Hatched

The scars of a trusted messenger are many, for the burden he carries is always heavy

ETSU TSUDI WAS SEATED on his throne. Around him, his three advisors were seated on wooden stools in a semi-circle. Before the Etsu, just outside his semi-circle of confidants, a little man lay prostrate with his forehead kissing the raffia carpet spread before him.

Beside this little man, was a sealed metal bucket which he had sworn contained a gift from an important admirer and distant loyal subject in the village of Zazzau.

"Baghadozi. My lord and master, Etsu of the Nupe empire," Masaba, head of the subordinate Nupe Kusapa clan, bowed low and began.

"Far be it from me to claim wisdom that is not mine. For all wisdom belongs to you as our ancestors have ordained. Therefore, please accept my words as mere considerations.

I do not think this man before us speaks truth and urge you to consider this an entrapment. Why would Zazzau send you anything good when we are yet to conquer them? I advise that this man be eliminated immediately, and we dispose of this so-called gift without even opening it."

"Masaba! Masaba! Masaba!" Saidu, head of the subordinate Nupe Batachi clan chided loudly. "I do not trust anything from Zazzau either. But does that mean that we should remain ignorant of the intentions of this man's master or the contents of the bucket?"

Saidu turned to Etsu Nupe and bowed low before speaking.

"*Baghadozi*. My lord and master. As Masaba has said, your judgement in this matter supersedes any counsel we may offer. That said, I advise that we further explore what this man has to say or present to you."

Etsu Tsudi observed both counselors with a wry smile. They were so often in conflict with each other. He was inclined to accept Saidu's counsel as he was indeed curious to know the contents of the bucket.

Furthermore, he rejected the supposition that he should somehow be apprehensive of a covert Zazzau plot. Etsu Tsudi feared no one! He turned to Mokwa as he most often did when there were opposing views from his counselors.

"And what do you think, my dear Mokwa?"

Mokwa, seated to the Etsu's immediate right, already had his answer. He bowed low to the Etsu as his colleagues had done.

"My lord and master. Your counsel is indeed final on this matter. However, my advice is that you should explore the purpose of this man's visit. You fear nothing and no one. So, what harm can come of mere exploration?"

Masaba frowned at Mokwa for a fleeting moment but quickly averted his face as Etsu Tsudi looked in his direction. Saidu, on the other hand, beamed at Mokwa.

Etsu Tsudi broke into a hearty laugh.

"Mokwa, you know me too well." He turned his attention to the prostrate figure before him. "Stranger, state your name and purpose once more. This time, you may present your gift."

The stranger lifted himself to a squat. He orated his practiced piece in a fearful voice.

"Your royal highness Etsu Tsudi, my name is Mutuwa Dole and I hold the position of high confidant of my master, Nikitau, husband to Princess Bakwa, the only offspring of Habe Nohi.

My master commanded that I undertake a sojourn to broker an allegiance with you and to declare his loyalty to you. As proof of his pledge of allegiance, I am instructed to present to you what I have in this bucket. Should you accept this, he promises he will henceforth send material gifts as well as important political and military..."

Mutuwa Dole barely finished delivering his rehearsed words in an audible voice. His voice trailed off as he choked on his words. He attempted to speak again but his voice trembled incoherently.

Etsu Tsudi glared at the man that cowered before him. He intended to sear dread into the man's soul.

This fool somehow found the courage to journey all this way south of the River Niger to deliver this message. A rat that shows itself when the hunter's torch burns brightly must be desperate for food or hopelessly naïve.

Etsu Tsudi smiled sardonically. He would gladly cure this man of any possible naivete.

Etsu Tsudi leaned forward to examine the bucket that contained the gift. It appeared ordinary enough. He turned to a guard by his side.

"Open it carefully and reveal its contents. Be prepared to relieve this man of his head should it contain anything dangerous." As the guard lifted the lid and dipped his hand into the bucket, Mutuwa Dole found his voice again.

"Your highness, what you are about to see, is the head of a Zazzau villager," he began. "My master has sent this to you as a symbolic gesture to demonstrate that he is willing to sacrifice Zazzau, he is willing to sacrifice everything for you, for your favor."

The guard retrieved Mustapha's decapitated head from the bucket. It had been soaked in honey to slow decay. He held it high for all to see as honey dripped down the macabre head into the bucket.

Masaba and Saidu gasped in horror.

Mokwa remained unfazed.

Etsu Tsudi let out a loud laugh like someone had just told a funny joke.

"Return that hideous head to the bucket at once!" he ordered once his mirth passed.

Etsu Tsudi rose abruptly from his throne and slowly approached Mutuwa Dole, who shrank backwards. Mokwa rose abruptly as well and advanced with Etsu Tsudi toward Mutuwa Dole, his sword unsheathed to protect his ruler should Mutuwa Dole attempt anything suspicious. The guard who had retrieved Mustapha's head from the bucket also tensed up beside Mutuwa Dole, prepared to attack if warranted.

When Etsu Tsudi reached Mutuwa Dole, he squatted so he could look him in the eye. Mutuwa Dole reluctantly met Etsu Tsudi's stare. His lips quivered, and he swallowed hard. His chest heaved rapidly.

Etsu Tsudi leaned forward, as close to Mutuwa Dole as he could. He breathed stale breath into Mutuwa Dole's lungs as he spoke in a low, slow growl.

"So, this master of yours, Nikitau, thinks he can somehow convince me of his loyalty by sending me the ugly head of a Zazzau commoner?"

Mutuwa Dole gulped and stuttered.

"Yes um...I swear on my ancestors. My master's intentions are honest and true. He has promised to send gifts and to provide you with valuable Zazzau information. If there is something else..."

Etsu Tsudi scowled and cut him off.

"Silence!"

Mutuwa Dole bit his words and looked down at the raffia mat. The silence that ensued was thick and the tension, palpable.

Etsu Tsudi slowly nibbled on his disfigured lip, allowing the tension to pervade for a while before he spoke again.

"Think before you respond to my next question Mutuwa Dole. If your answer displeases me. I shall have your head instantly."

Mutuwa Dole gulped. He looked like a man staring into the face of death.

Etsu Tsudi paused again, then asked, "What does your master desire in exchange for my blessing, in exchange for my favor?"

Mutuwa Dole squirmed and squeezed his thighs together like a man pressed to empty his bladder. His reply tumbled out of his lips before he even realized he had started speaking.

"Princess Bakwa has recently conceived a child. My master fears that this child might turn out to be male. If this happens, he will never get the chance to rule Zazzau. He is hopeful that you might someday help him ascend the throne."

Silence followed for a time that seemed like forever. Mutuwa Dole could restrain his bladder no longer. A warm liquid began to trickle down his inner thigh. He squeezed his laps tighter.

"Give me your hand." Etsu Tsudi said. His voice was serene. But his eyes, his eyes were cold.

Mutuwa Dole hesitated. But his resistance only lasted a blink. He felt his right hand roughly seized by the guard beside him and presented to the Etsu.

Mutuwa Dole began to cry out loud and beg for mercy.

Etsu Tsudi, in one swift move, produced a dagger from the side of his wrapper, pinned Mutuwa Dole's hand to the raffia mat and stabbed the center of his palm.

Blood spurted where the dagger made its mark.

Mutuwa Dole hollered in pain and his eyes rolled backwards in his head.

"This will only get worse if you do not speak truth to me," Etsu Tsudi warned through clenched teeth, his eyes vicious. "I give you one last chance to speak truth."

Etsu Tsudi yanked the dagger out and violently stabbed his hand again. Mutuwa Dole again screamed in agony and swore on his ancestors that he spoke nothing but truth.

Etsu Tsudi paused to observe the little man writhing in agony before him, constrained by the grip of his powerful guard and the blade pinning his palm to the ground.

Perhaps the man was telling the truth. But, for good measure, and to cure the man of all naivete about the extent of his ruthlessness, Etsu Tsudi lifted the blade one last time and brought it crashing down into his palm.

Mutuwa Dole screamed again and lost consciousness.

Etsu Tsudi pulled his dagger out from Mutuwa Dole's palm, wiped his blade on his guard's pants and turned to Mokwa.

"I think we just gained an important spy in Zazzau. Get Majiya to attend to this man's wounds and send him back to Nikitau with this message. 'Your servant returns to you with his life as evidence that your intentions are understood. The substance of your loyalty, however, will be tested by the value of the information you provide.'"

CHAPTER EIGHTEEN

Costly Alliance

Choice is a luxury. Necessity drives a quick decision

HABE NOHI SPENT MANY days following his return from Katsina mulling over the costly prospect of his desired alliance with Sarki Ibrahim Maje.

For a short while, he considered journeying to Songhai himself to propose an alliance with Askia Daud instead. But he quickly discarded this idea for he knew quite well that a direct alliance with Songhai would come at a cost he could not afford.

Habe Nohi was not prepared to abandon his faith in his Zazzau ancestors to convert to Islam like Sarki Ibrahim Maje had done. It would be an abomination to Zazzau's cherished heritage and future.

As Habe Nohi contemplated the cost of his proposed alliance, he also grew concerned for Amina's safety.

What guarantee would there be that the Sarki would be good to Amina in the long term? Obviously, the Sarki would not violate terms of the agreement or publicly humiliate Amina. But who would know what was done in secret? How could he be certain that Amina would be protected in a foreign village?

Habe Nohi loved his beloved granddaughter's fierce spirit and shrank from the imagination that she might be maltreated in a foreign land.

Increasingly restless and less inclined to discuss such a personal matter with all his noble council men, Habe Nohi opted to seek counsel from the one council man he trusted above all others, Madaki Zaki.

The two men, escorted by a host of armed guards, were taking an evening stroll in the royal garden behind the palace dwellings. They walked together in silence for a while, each observing the well-manicured shrubs that formed a wall on either side of the bare pathway they were traversing. Madaki Zaki examined his ruler's troubled face with great concern.

Finally, Habe Nohi spoke. "Madaki Zaki. How is the reinforcement recruitment process going for our Sojojin Zazzau?"

"Your royal highness, my esteemed Habe. It is progressing very well. We are about to begin training the latest batch of recruits. I will leave no stone unturned to ensure our military capabilities are as potent as can possibly be in readiness for any future invasions."

Habe Nohi paused to pat Madaki Zaki on the back, an approving smile capturing his features despite his troubled mind.
"I have full confidence in you, Madaki Zaki. Our Sojojin would be lost without your able leadership."

"You are too kind to me, Habe. It is your leadership that gives us pride and keeps us fearless," Madaki Zaki replied with a smile and bowed.

Habe Nohi gathered his babban riga about him and resumed his walk. They again walked in silence for a while.

Madaki Zaki finally asked. "My Habe, your royal highness. It appears something troubles you. Might I be of some assistance?"

Habe Nohi paused again and faced his supreme commander. He smiled affectionately and nodded slowly.

"Madaki Zaki, perceptive as ever. Indeed, water does not turn sour without a cause. I do have a bothersome concern that has been souring my mood for quite some time now."

"Ah, I sensed it, my Habe. If it is appropriate, do share this concern with me and by the power of our ancestors, I will do my best to help alleviate it."

Habe Nohi nodded in agreement. "It is appropriate, Madaki Zaki and I will share it. My concern is for Amina. I have previously shared with you that I intend to give her in marriage to Sarki Ibrahim Maje as a seal of our alliance with Katsina. Have I not?"

Madaki Zaki's eyebrows were furrowed in thought. "Indeed, my Habe, you have shared this with me. Is there a problem? Does Sarki Ibrahim Maje not value the beauty and gracefulness of young Princess Amina?"

Habe Nohi shook his head. "Actually Madaki, on the contrary, he is quite taken with her beauty. But I am worried about her safety in a foreign land. She is still only a child and has no way to defend herself.

Although she will have personal guards accompany her from our village once she is married, I remain concerned as to how to guarantee her long-term security."

Madaki Zaki was quiet, his eyes fixed on the bare pathway as though he was willing a solution to appear from beneath the surface. When he spoke, he kept his eyes averted from Habe Nohi's.

"My Habe, first, I must ask for your permission and that you forgive my boldness for the suggestion I am about to make." Habe Nohi, eager to receive any valuable counsel quickly granted consent.

"Habe Nohi," Madaki Zaki began, this time looking up to meet Habe Nohi's gaze. "For a while now, I have harbored a persistent feeling that your beloved Princess Amina has a destiny that is unique, a destiny that is different from that of all females in Zazzau.

Please do not be dismayed that you are allowing your granddaughter to venture into harm's way as I firmly believe her destiny is secure in the hands of our ancestors. If I may be so bold as to suggest the unusual..."

Madaki Zaki's voice trailed off and he swallowed hard, his eyes suddenly falling away from Habe Nohi's gaze.

Habe Nohi was puzzled. What could this counsel be that caused such a courageous warrior to choke on his own words? "Speak your mind and do not hold back, Madaki Zaki!" Habe Nohi ordered impatiently.

"My suggestion is that you allow Princess Amina to train as a warrior with our latest batch of recruits. I realize this is highly unusual and..."

"Enough!" Habe Nohi thundered, anger flashing in his eyes. "I will ignore the foolishness of your suggestion only because I gave permission for you to utter it. How could an experienced warrior such as yourself suggest such a thing? Would you have her trade her grace and beauty for a sword and shield?"

Madaki Zaki shook his head, then he bowed his head in deference and tried one more time. "My Habe, your royal highness. Have I not served you faithfully and honorably for many years now? Am I not your chief warrior who has stood by your side or gone on your command to battle on many occasions?

Please forgive the apparent absurdity of my suggestion but know that I have not made this suggestion in haste. Please permit to me to make this case once and for all and hereafter I will forever be silent on the matter."

"Very well, make it brief" Habe Nohi said, a deep frown still etched on his face.

Madaki Zaki continued, his head still bowed but his eyes lifted to meet Habe Nohi's eyes. "My Habe, I know it is not news to you or me that Princess Amina has always been keenly interested in the Sojojin Zazzau and that she has always demonstrated a deep love of adventure.

What has intrigued me about the princess more recently is her courage and fortitude. When she saved that village girl the other day, she did so against insurmountable odds not merely posed by the girl's attacker but also by the rugged terrain.

My Habe, I will spare you the details of that escapade but let me say this, the courage I saw her display is rare even among my well-trained warriors. I can only imagine how wonderful it would be to have such courage in a body that is trained at the highest level. If you permit me to train her, I promise you on my life that you will have nothing to fear for her safety in Katsina."

Habe Nohi had listened, but only in adherence to his principle of open opinions. He had no intention of allowing Amina train as a warrior. The mere thought of such a thing occurring caused him to cringe to his core.

"Thank you Madaki Zaki," he grunted. "Your counsel is noted for consideration."

♦♦♦

Amina was sound asleep on her mud-brick bed. Suddenly, she began to rouse to a ticklish sensation on her left thigh. She initially batted it away sleepily, believing the sensation to be caused by a worrisome bug.

But the sensation persisted and intensified. Drowsy, Amina moved her hand to her thigh and felt the sensation creeping up to between her legs. Her hand touched on skin, warm...a hand. Alarmed, Amina jumped to a sitting position, carving knife in hand, dagger end drawn.

Her assailant was caught unawares by the drawn knife which Amina had hitherto concealed under her. He fell backwards on the floor and Amina leapt onto him like a cat, sticking the pointed edge of the knife close to his neck. His black turban came undone.

Amina gasped. "Sarki Ibrahim Maje!" she exclaimed. Her hand trembled and the carving knife dropped.

The Sarki seized the moment and pushed the helpless girl to the ground. Amina began to cry for help as he pinned her to the ground and feverishly ripped her clothes off, laughing at her feeble attempts to stop him.

Habe Nohi sat up on his bed drenched in sweat. This was the second night in a row he had suffered such a dream since speaking with Madaki Zaki about his concern for Amina's safety.

As he swung groggily out of bed, he called for a servant to bring him water for his parched throat. He vowed he would not suffer such a terrible dream again if he could help it.

CHAPTER NINETEEN

Nupe Clan Annexations

It is human nature to dominate. But how to dominate, therein lies the choice

ON A LENGTHY STRIP along the northern banks of the great River Niger, a plethora of mud, thatch-roofed huts were lined symmetrically in rows and columns.

Bordering these huts to the south was a deep forest and marshlands that stretched far and wide, parallel to the great Niger. There was bustling activity in and around this settlement of huts which was the Nupe clan of Bini.

The morning was still quite young. The air around had a certain freshness to it, imbued with moisture conjured from the nearby river by the virgin breeze that wafted across the surface every now and then.

Blue smoke, tall as a mountain, rose from several cooking pots with bottoms aflame on the muddy shores close to the river front. Before each of these pots, bare-breasted women sat, whipping up favorite family breakfast recipes such as fried bean cakes, boiled yams with palm oil stew or lentil soup filled with fresh fish from the Niger's depths.

On the river, close to the shore, industrious fishermen stood upright in long, thin, wooden canoes casting wide nets into the Niger. They were hopeful for an early morning catch.

Children, naked and unashamed, ran in circles on the muddy shores, squealing as they evaded one another in friendly games of catch.

Some men, especially the alcoholics, still slumbered within their family huts. Other men, early risers but nonetheless lazy, slouched on mats or wooden chairs either watching their wives prepare the family breakfast on the river shore or dozing off to the gentle caress of the early morning breeze.

The idyllic innocence of the morning was suddenly violated by the horrified hollering of a village scout racing towards the settlement from the forest behind.

"Etsu's warriors are coming! They are coming!"

The bare footed scout was running like one hunted by wild animals, having sacrificed his weapons in haste to reach the settlement and alert his fellow clan citizens of the impending danger.

The scout got within a few hundred feet of the Bini settlement before his life was brutally ended by the machete of a masked horseman who rode past him in a frenzy.

The machete severed the scout's head, sending it, with mortified eyes bulging, high into the air and drawing a fountain of blood from the headless body that collapsed in the opposite direction. The severed head crashed onto the earth and rolled a few times before it was crushed by a stampede of masked horsemen riding alongside and behind the murderous leader.

The people of Bini had not much time to run or hide. The horseback invaders descended upon the village, corralling all they could find and slaughtering the few men who dared to put up a feeble resistance.

The quiet settlement erupted in cries of terror and pleas for mercy as the invaders rampantly rounded everyone up. As machetes and axes flashed, blood spurted, and clan citizens fell, the brave Bini warriors who dared to resist buckled and surrendered their feeble weapons in total submission.

Soon the entire settlement had been arrested. Women and children were pressed together, huddled on the shore like fish caught in a net. The men were gathered separately and forced to kneel in rows with heads bowed and arms behind their backs.

The leader of the gang of horsemen dismounted from his horse, bloody machete in hand and slowly removed his mask; a macabre construct with a triangular wooden face, horns that spiraled skywards, and a protruding nose sharp and extended like a bird's beak.

The leader cast a grave look across the vast array of villagers now subdued before his horsemen who had also dismounted.

"Which one of you common rats is Chief Edegi, the one whom my emissary has been liaising with?" the leader asked in a loud voice, surveying the rows of captured men with a contemptuous sneer.

It did not surprise him that the chief of the village was not easily recognizable amongst the group of kneeling men. The coward would have hastily stripped himself of all royal trappings in order to appear as a commoner.

The question was greeted with silence from the men and wailing from the women and children.

The action that followed was swift and sudden. The leader lifted his bloody machete high and landed it with great force on the Bini man kneeling closest to him.

The victim's skull burst open like a shattered coconut, drawing blood which splattered like raindrops onto the men nearby. Horrified gasps rang out from the men even as the limp body of the slain one collapsed onto them like a branch severed from a tree.

The wailing from the women and children intensified upon beholding the horrific sight. A few women and children, next of kin to the slain man, threw themselves on the muddy ground wailing and consumed by abject grief and terror.

"For each question that meets silence as a reply, one shall die. Now, I ask again, which one of you common rats is Chief Edegi?"

A man in the front row of the kneeling men sprang up, his eyes steely and unblinking.

"Etsu Tsudi, please forgive me for being slow to respond. I am Chief Edegi."

Etsu Tsudi walked up to the man, slowly examining him from head to toe. This man looked young and vibrant, nothing like the aged Bini leader his emissary had described. This man was husky like a henchman, more likely a chief's assistant than a chief himself.

Etsu Tsudi laughed a wicked laugh, then nibbled on his lip, clenching his teeth as he did so.

"Ok, Chief Edegi," Etsu Tsudi said, patting the man's back, then turning his face towards the clustered women and children on the opposite side of the men, he said.

"My men here have now seen how beautiful your subjects are; the women of Bini. Your women have lovely skins and supple breasts. I can see my men are eager to comfort these mournful but beautiful women of Bini. It is indeed a shame to have such beautiful women drowning in sorrow while there are so many virile men around capable of comforting them."

Etsu Tsudi paused and began to pace, his head hung and his eyes surveying the captives before him, appearing to be deep in thought. Soon he stopped, looked up at the group of kneeling men, and continued.

"This is what I have decided. Until the real Chief Edegi identifies himself, I will permit my warriors to comfort as many women here as they are able.

My warriors will do this, right here and right now before your children and the husbands of these women. We will all observe just how skilled my warriors are at comforting women. If the real Chief Edegi does not identify himself, then let the disgrace of Bini's virtuous women forever be upon him and his household."

Etsu Tsudi had hardly finished speaking these words when a roar of lust filled euphoria erupted amongst his warriors. The masked men promptly descended upon the helpless females, each one grabbing as many wailing women as he could, beginning to rip off the scant loincloths that had so far protected virtue in the community.

"Please stop!"

The voice that cut loudly through the ensuing mayhem was stern and authoritative.

Etsu Tsudi turned sharply in the direction of the voice, a crafty smile on his face.

An aging man, tall and slim with a shaved head and sad eyes stood up in the middle of the cowering men.

"Etsu Tsudi, I beseech you by the mercies of our ancestors. I beseech you for your dearly departed mother's sake. Please have mercy upon us."

Etsu Tsudi held up his hand to halt the assault his men had begun, much to their chagrin. Groans of disappointment permeated the air as the men released the women they had grabbed. These women rushed back to embrace their petrified children, tearful but relieved that they had been spared violation.

Etsu Tsudi's crafty smile turned into a self-satisfied one. He had known his methods would work, as always.

"Step forward Chief Edegi."

Chief Edegi was aging but physically fit. He boldly complied, slowly easing himself through the crowd of his kneeling subjects until he stood before Etsu Tsudi. He bowed his head in obeisance and dropped to his knees.

Etsu Tsudi observed the man kneeling before him with great curiosity.

What false spirit had misled this cowardly ruler into thinking he could continue to defy the Etsu of Nupe and never suffer the consequences?

For some time now, the chief had stubbornly refused for his village to be annexed as subjects of Etsu Tsudi. He had claimed he saw no benefit in allying Bini to an empire that did not yet exist. He had expressed to the Etsu's emissary that he was vehemently opposed to Bini being taxed by Etsu Tsudi.

Etsu Tsudi wondered if Chief Edegi, now kneeling before his bloody blade regretted such resistance. He wondered if the chief would submit or fight to salvage some pride before his people.

"Now you choose to beg for mercy?" Etsu Tsudi asked. He turned sharply to a man who had been standing behind him, quiet but observant, all along.

"Mokwa, did I not send my emissary several times to a certain Chief Edegi of the Bini people asking that he join the Nupe confederation under me, pledge fealty and pay tribute? Did we not promise great benefits to be enjoyed from allying with our Nupe empire?"

Mokwa's face displayed some unease.

"Yes, my lord Etsu. I must say, as always, you are correct, and your memory is as sound as it is blessed by our ancestors. However, if my lord would permit me, I beseech you to show mercy upon these errant people. They are also the people of your deceased mother who now watches over us with our ancestors."

"You hear that Bini people?" Etsu Tsudi projected, looking around him at the many that cowered before him in fear. "You hear that? My advisor Mokwa asks for mercy on your behalf. Mercy, he says."

Etsu Tsudi paused as though considering Mokwa's intercession. Then he exclaimed, exploding spittle like venom from his lips.

"Mercy! I...am...merciful!

I gave your chief here a choice. Join me, pay homage and tribute and I will make you a great clan. I sent a clear message to him. I said, together, we will expand the Nupe empire as far as the Maghreb in the north and beyond the Igala in the south.

But Chief Edegi foolishly refused. Your chief chose to deny you all greatness. He chose to deny you the benefits beyond Bini that only I can give to you."

Etsu Tsudi stopped speaking and looked down with disdain at Chief Edegi's shiny head bowed before him. "So, tell me, mighty and powerful Chief Edegi who dares refuse me. Why should I let you live?"

Chief Edegi spoke, his face still downcast, his body trembling from shame, humiliation, and from the chilly morning breeze. He stretched out both hands cupped in submission towards Etsu Tsudi.

"*Bagbadozi.* My lord and master, Etsu of the Nupe empire. Have mercy upon me and your people. I see now the foolishness of my ways. I pledge fealty to you now and forever and only ask that you mercifully spare me and my people.

My people will be your people in times of war and in peace. Our lands and produce will be yours in times of war and peace. We shall willingly join the Nupe empire and repel all who would resist us within or outside the empire."

Etsu Tsudi beamed. He looked around the entire village with great satisfaction. The Bini clan was now truly conquered and subservient to him. Ever since the Zazzau defeat, he had grown weary of Mokwa's proposed diplomatic efforts to convert the clans. He was pleased to see he had made the right decision to force allegiance. Now he would have more men join him to coerce other unyielding clans into submission.

Etsu Tsudi returned his gaze to the kneeling chief before him.

"Let this be a warning to you and to all who might think it wise to oppose me. Refuse or oppose me henceforth and you shall die a miserable death. Chief Edegi, for your insolence, you shall die today. Your wives shall become mine and your children shall be taken as my slaves."

Upon hearing this, an aging woman burst into loud wailing. She suddenly broke free from the crowd of women and children and raced to Etsu Tsudi, falling flat and hard on her face when she reached him.

Mokwa, alert as ever, had raised his machete high to protect the Etsu from a possible surprise attack but stalled as the Etsu Tsudi held up his hand.

"Etsu Tsudi, our lord and master," the woman gushed through her anguish. "Please have mercy on my husband, the chief, and us, your loyal Bini subjects. I beseech you by the mercies of our ancestors. Do not take us or our children from our home, from our people. Please show mercy. Please... I beg of you."

Feeling gratified by the power he now wielded, Etsu Tsudi examined the mortified female that lay half naked on the muddy ground before his feet. He imagined she was the eldest wife of

Chief Edegi. The royalty of this clan now lay prostrate at his feet in complete submission.

Etsu Tsudi had intended to make a public show of Chief Edegi's death as a warning to all who would oppose him. But he sensed now that he had served the warning already. He now saw an opportunity to evoke gratitude from the people by showing mercy.

Etsu Tsudi sheathed his machete and drew a small dagger from his leather waist belt. With this dagger, he sliced one of Chief Edegi's outstretched palms drawing blood and a yelp of pain from the bowed chief.

"Let the scar from this wound be a warning to you Chief Edegi. But let it also serve as a seal of your allegiance to me. If you ever break this allegiance, I will bring upon you and the Bini people a wrath so great, you will wish I had not spared you this day when you begged for my mercy."

Etsu Tsudi looked up again at the cowering crowd of Bini villagers and projected in a loud voice.

"My Bini people, from this day henceforth, I declare that we are one. I am your ruler and you are my loyal subjects, worthy of my protection and my provision. As a sign of my commitment to your prosperity, I declare that no taxes in food, substance, or gold, shall be collected from you for the first sixty days of your joining the Nupe empire. I also declare that a generous portion of the spoils from our first conquest will be given to you as a reward."

Humiliated but relieved and grateful for Etsu Tsudi's mercy, Chief Edegi nodded vigorously in agreement. Clasping his wounded palm in his other hand for some measure of comfort, he declared in a loud voice.

"My Bini people, let us hail Etsu Tsudi for his mercy and benevolence. Etsu Tsudi is truly *Baghadozi.*"

The captives replied in unison. "Etsu Tsudi is truly *Baghadozi.* We thank you for your mercy, our lord and master."

As suddenly as the invasion began, it concluded. The invaders rode off towards the next clan to be subjugated, leaving a settlement that had begun the day joyful, now broken and in dire need of healing.

CHAPTER TWENTY

Amina – A Warrior Emerges

That which one is truly capable of may forever remain a mystery

"RISE WARRIOR, COME WITH me!" The voice was Madaki Zaki's. *To whom is he speaking?* Amina wondered as she struggled to rouse herself from sleep. The loud thud of a metal sword and shield landing on the bare earth floor close to her mud-brick bed had startled her.

"I said, rise!" Madaki Zaki commanded again.

Amina roused, confused. Madaki Zaki had never spoken to her in such a stern manner. She rubbed her eyes, adjusting to the semi dark hut barely illuminated by the early rays of sunlight streaking in through crevices in the thatched door and windows.

She glanced at her mother's mud-brick bed a few feet away. Princess Bakwa, now visibly pregnant, was wide awake, sitting with her legs spread on her bed for comfort, her hands on her protruding stomach. She remained silent, like a ghost in the hut.

"I don't understand," Amina said, her eyes now wide. She looked from her mother to Madaki Zaki, who was fully kitted in dashiki warrior attire with his sword in kilt and shield in hand.

"Do you, or do you not desire to serve Zazzau as a warrior?"

Amina's eyes lit up like a spark of fire from the clash of two rocks together. She felt her heart quicken with excitement. She glanced at her mother again, her eyes asking the question.

Princess Bakwa nodded in the semi-darkness, then looked away towards one of the two thatch-veiled windows in the hut. Amina quickly surmised, from her mother's demeanor, that this was her grandfather's decision. Her mother's consent had been coerced. But she did not care.

She leapt to her feet, grabbing the metal sword Madaki Zaki had tossed to her only to drop it as it weighed quite a lot more than she anticipated. Madaki Zaki shook his head and smiled.

"Clearly, there is much to teach you, my young princess. Quick, put this dashiki on and let us be on our way." He threw a folded dashiki uniform at Amina and she caught it before darting into an inner room to change.

Moments later, Amina joined Madaki Zaki on his horse and they rode together, against the cold Harmattan wind, to the Zazzau training valley which also served as the trainee parade ground.

As they journeyed, Madaki Zaki spoke to Amina, confirming her assumption that Habe Nohi had authorized her training, though he would not share why.

Madaki Zaki also informed her that an important condition for effective training was that she be viewed as an equal to all the young aspiring warriors she would be training with.

"But what have the aspiring warriors been told, Madaki? They are not likely to accept a female joining their ranks. How do I make them accept me?" Amina's face clouded with worry.

"They have been told that you are a mere commoner joining their ranks, a test case for training female warriors authorized by Habe Nohi himself. No one will recognize you since you have always worn a veil in public. And you are forbidden from disclosing who you are. Don't worry, no harm shall befall you. I will make certain of it."

Amina was not convinced she would be safe. And, she could not quite imagine how it would feel to be treated like an ordinary girl. But she did not care to debate the topic further lest she ruin this opportunity to become a warrior.

They rode in silence for a while.

"I would like them to call me Aisha," Amina said, opting for her maidservant's name as an alias.

Madaki Zaki nodded in agreement.

As the wind whipped against her cheeks, she held on to Madaki Zaki as tightly as she could, her heart filled with excitement akin to a child headed to a village party.

When Madaki Zaki's horse neared the trainee parade ground, Amina saw in the semi-darkness of the early morning, that the ground was already occupied by a significant number of people.

As they drew nearer still, she detected that the people on the ground were young men clothed as she was in dashiki uniform. These men stood at attention, braving the cold, whistling wind that swept through the barren parade ground.

She and Madaki Zaki arrived at the parade ground. As they dismounted from his horse, Madaki Zaki observed Amina's puzzled face and he explained.

"This is your warrior class. They are ninety-nine of Zazzau's most promising young men. Today, you join them as the hundredth member and the first ever female trainee. Now, go and take your place in their formation. I have no doubt you will do me and your grandfather proud."

Amina's excitement peaked as she walked towards her warrior class. But she felt nervous too. What if her male counterparts did not accept her? How would she prove to them that she was worthy of being one of them?

Had she not been so wrapped in her nervous rumination, she might have noticed that one of the stoic warriors in the front row had stuck his foot out just enough to trip her.

Amina tripped and fell, stretching out her hands just in time to break her fall and keep from hurting her jaw on the hard ground. She rose sharply and instinctively accosted the one who dared to prank her, a princess of Zazzau.

"How dare you?"

Laughter erupted from the trainees in the front row. However, not all trainees enjoyed the prank. One stepped out of formation and boldly reprimanded the others.

"Musa! Stop it. She could have been hurt. This is beneath you."

Amina recognized the voice and her face softened. She was surprised to see Mahmud here, among the ranks of the aspiring warriors. Why hadn't he told her he was enlisting in the Sojojin Zazzau? Her anger melted, and she smiled at him, mouthing her gratitude for his support. He returned her smile before Madaki Zaki's voice interrupted the moment.

"Aisha, I asked you to join the warriors, not to cower before them!" Madaki Zaki thundered.

The one whom Mahmud had referred to as Musa - a tall, muscular male with jaws like stone edges, taunted her further.
"Yes, little girl, don't be so fickle. We are here to train as warriors, not play girlish games in the dust."

"Silence, Musa!" Madaki Zaki thundered. "One more word out of you and you will spend the day in the prison pit. Is that clear?"

Musa recoiled. "Yes sir."

Amina dusted her dashiki and promptly assumed her place in formation as the hundredth member of the group. She did not have to wonder anymore how an ordinary girl would be treated by this group. She had no plan to counter such ill treatment – not yet anyway.

"Hear me, warrior trainees," Madaki Zaki began in a loud voice. Beside him, Ahmed, his assistant, and several other Sojojin Zazzau warriors stood, ready to serve as training instructors. Madaki Zaki continued.

"You all have been training for a few days now. Aisha, who joins you today will make your class special. She will make your class historic if you all work together towards the common goal of becoming worthy members of the Sojojin Zazzau."

Amina cringed at his words. Was Madaki Zaki setting her up as a target with the group?

Madaki Zaki was still speaking.

"You must treat Aisha as your equal. Our elders say a man does not stick a knife into his stomach and then go out and boast about it. If you do not wholeheartedly accept Aisha, it is the same as sticking a knife in your own stomach for disunity will eventually lead to your downfall.

Henceforth, you will train together, fight together, live together and if necessary, die together as warriors for the sake of our beloved Zazzau."

The first day of training did not go as Amina had imagined. She had expected to begin learning to handle a sword, a spear, a shield, or any weapon of sorts.

But the warrior initiates did no weapons training at all. They were ordered to run up and down one of the tall hills in the Zazzau Valley all day, stopping only to eat and for brief water breaks.

Those who were slowest and lagged suffered the cruelty of the Zazzau trainers' whips as they were chased up the hill. And, when the laggards eventually reached the summit to join the rest of the initiates, the entire troop was punished for the struggles of the laggards.

"You live and die together!" Madaki Zaki's words thundered in the initiates ears prior to, and, at the end of each race. Amina was one of the laggards that struggled to keep up with her male counterparts. Whenever she slowed her run, a trainer would come charging after her with a dried leather whip. Amina ran until her legs turned to rubber and she felt certain she would collapse and die from exhaustion.

Long after the sun had resigned on the first training day, the initiates finally got to rest, each retiring gratefully to one of two large mobile tents erected for them on the far south end of the training valley. Each initiate had been provided with essentials - a raffia mat, a water pot, and a designated sleeping space in the tent.

Amina noted with regret that Mahmud was not assigned to her tent. She had hardly found the time to speak to him throughout the hectic training day. Lunch and dinner had been consumed without relish or savor.

She determined she would connect with him one way or the other. But that is tomorrow's concern, she conceded, barely reaching her mat before collapsing into a deep sleep.

Madaki Zaki had ensured that she was afforded a bit of privacy from her male counterparts - a spot at the far end of the tent with a makeshift curtain.

Amina had not slept for long when she was awakened by a raucous occurring right outside her tent curtain. She sat up and rubbed her eyes, adjusting to the dull lighting providing by the oil lamps along the internal perimeter of the tent.

Amina sighted Mahmud standing with his arms outstretched to prevent the advancement of certain aggressors, Musa and two initiates. Musa was head and shoulders taller, and bigger than Mahmud. The two initiates were roughly the same size as Mahmud.

Fighting against Musa alone, Mahmud might have had a small chance to do some damage. But against the three of them, he stood no chance and would be stupid to even try. They bore down on him, pushing and shoving him.

"Leave her alone," Mahmud protested. "For our ancestors' sake, she is a female. What did you expect? We should give her time."

"She slows us down Mahmud and each time we get punished for it," Musa countered. "Why are you so keen on defending her? Do you not see that a female warrior puts all warriors at risk in battle?"

"It is only a terrible idea if we make it so," Mahmud retorted. He was being forced backwards into Amina's curtain as the trio pushed and shoved him.

Amina leapt to her feet, catching them by surprise. She drew her dagger, poised like a cat to defend herself.

"Mahmud!" she yelled. "Step aside. Let these cowards come to me. I will send any one of them who dares touch me to his ancestors tonight."

Mahmud spun around, his eyes widening with apprehension upon seeing the dagger in her hand.

"And what do you think you will do with that dagger, small girl?" Musa spat on the ground. He parted her makeshift curtain and moved towards her.

Suddenly, his two companions capitalized on Mahmud's momentary distraction and seized him, restraining him as tightly as they could.

Amina was now face to face with Musa.

Other initiates in the tent had awoken as well. They now watched the situation with keen interest.

"Drop the knife. You don't need it."

Amina looked quickly around her and back to Musa's advancing figure. *Who said that?* She had heard that voice as clear as she could hear Musa's, but it did not seem to come from anyone in the room. She felt an overwhelming impulse to drop the knife.

She complied, tossing it as far away as she could, towards her water pot.

"I don't need it," she said out loud, echoing the words she had heard to Musa.

Musa laughed, as did his cohorts who still restrained Mahmud tightly.

"First you assume in your childish mind that you can fight me with the dagger. Now you add stupidity to your childishness by presuming you can fight me without it? Are you blind or something?"

Musa paused and glanced at his cohorts, his eyes mocking her action. They sneered and urged him to teach her a lesson she would not forget in a hurry.

Musa returned his focus to Amina.

"It seems you are eager to add a heavy beating to your training and I would be very happy to grant your desire."

"What are you doing Aisha?" Mahmud asked, clearly alarmed but careful not to address her by her real name.

Amina wasn't sure what she was doing either. But she felt empowered, excited even, like one propelled by a powerful wind. This was going to be ok. She did not know how. It just was.

In a flash, Musa pounced.

Although he moved quickly, Amina saw his movement slowly unfold. She found she had enough time to observe his movement and react.

She saw his left-handed punch coming to the right of her face and dodged leftwards. Another punch, right-handed was aimed at her stomach. She jumped backwards, avoiding a direct hit.

The impact of a left and right combination swing and miss cost Musa his footing and he found himself falling forwards into Amina. She again jumped backwards to avoid his head ramming into her stomach. As she did so, she saw an opportunity and took it, raining two quick blows to the back of his head.

Musa yelped as the blows landed and he crashed to the ground. Amina, her body tensed with adrenalin and rage, leapt onto him like a frenzied cat and began raining successive blows on his face.

Her fists were much smaller than his and she could not strike as hard as he could. But what she lacked in power, she compensated for in momentum, accuracy and quantity.

Musa tried to shove her off him but couldn't. As he struggled helplessly under her, his face contorted into a bloodied mess. He began pleading for mercy, blood stemming from his bruised lips.

The entire tent was motionless and stunned. Mouths hung open and eyes glared in awe of their female counterpart. No one had expected this. No one could believe what they were witnessing.

"Say you are sorry. Say you will never disrespect me again. Say it now!" Amina yelled at Musa and spat in his face as she pounded away. Her voice was hoarse, her eyes and fists were blood red. The strength in her body at this point was foreign to her but potent.

Musa apologized and begged again and again.

Finally, some stunned onlookers broke from their state of frozen disbelief and began to yell for Amina to stop lest she kill him.

Others, enjoying the show, urged Amina on. One starting a chant in honor of her and on cue, several others joined in the catchy tune.

"A-yee-sha fight! A-yee-sha fight! Woman like a man, fight! Woman like a man fight!"

Mahmud's restrainers let go of him and rushed to save Musa. Mahmud stood back, awestruck.

As Musa's companions reached the duo on the floor, yelling at Amina to leave Musa alone but hesitant to interfere, a bold voice thundered through the tent.

"Silence! The lot of you!"

Madaki Zaki walked briskly in with a long, polished wooden rod firmly in one hand and the other holding up the edge of the sleeping wrapper he had tied around his waist. There was a riot of shuffling feet as the fight spectators now dived back onto their raffia mats, pretending to be asleep.

Musa's friends, and Mahmud, quickly straightened upright with eyes forward. They stood still, at attention like statues.

Madaki Zaki walked towards Amina, glancing at Musa cradling his bloodied face on the floor. Amina had ceased her attack on Musa when she heard Madaki Zaki's voice.

As Madaki Zaki approached Amina, she slowly rose and stood at attention like Mahmud and the other two. Her fists, colored with Musa's blood, were clenched by her side. Her chest heaved heavily up and down as the last vestiges of the furor and fervor she had felt dissipated.

"What is going on here Aisha?" Madaki Zaki asked in a loud voice. "What is the reason for this impudence shown in my training camp?"

Madaki Zaki again glanced to the floor where Musa lay crumpled, nursing his wounds. He had not, at first, comprehended the extent of the damage Amina inflicted because she had been atop Musa when he first observed the scene. Now he saw Musa in full view and his eyes widened in astonishment.

"Whomever helped you do this to Musa will feel the wrath of my chastening rod tonight. Aisha, point out your helpers, now!" Madaki Zaki boomed, shaking his rod at her.

Amina cast a defiant glance at her vanquished foe and felt a rueful tinge. Like one delivered of a devil's desire, her now steady state of mind was seized by a sense of wonder and astonishment.

How had she managed to handily beat Musa? How had she managed to inflict such damage on him?

Musa's friends did not wait for her to assume culpability. They immediately began to cast blame but were silenced by Madaki Zaki who was studying Amina closely.

He moved close to her until his face was a mere hair-length away from hers. He peered into her blood-colored eyes and face. She held his gaze, her eyes betrayed no relief or remorse, no shame or sorrow. He repeated his words in a quiet but no less threatening voice.

"Aisha, I will ask one last time. Who helped you do this? You will do well to tell me the truth or your punishment will be much worse."

Amina blurted out the words without even thinking. "I did this, with the help of my ancestors. My ancestors helped me show this pitiful brute that my strength lies not in my physical power but in a higher power."

Madaki Zaki retained his gaze on her but narrowed his eyes.

"Ok Aisha, you think this is a joke? Very well, follow me. We shall see if the ancestors will save you from my wrath tonight." He grabbed Amina's wrist. As he turned to exit, he addressed one of Musa's two cohorts.

"Kudi, fetch our nurse, Mama Sojojin, from the trainer tents and ask her to attend to Musa's wounds. Everyone else, including you fools pretending to be asleep, I will tolerate no further disturbance tonight. If there is any additional commotion tonight or any other night for that matter, I will make certain that you all forget how to even sleep at all."

Amina spent part of the night under interrogation in Madaki Zaki's tent. He relentlessly demanded that she give a truthful account of what had occurred that night.

Each time she replied, she provided the same explanation - a narration of the night's events with an emphasis of the somewhat indescribable fortitude and strength she experienced which could only have come from her ancestors.

After Amina explained the details for the umpteenth time, Madaki revealed that he would not punish her because he had promised to keep her safe. Amina was relieved to escape with a mere reprimand.

Madaki Zaki admonished her to report, to him, any future incidents that might occur, instead of engaging in a fight.

Training resumed the next day. Amina awoke sore and limp but resolved, as Madaki Zaki commanded, to put the Musa episode behind her and commit herself fully to training.

Although she was determined to follow through with her resolve, her initiate counterparts made it difficult. They remained in awe of her and repeated the chant from the night before, whenever possible, in hushed tones.

"A-yee-sha fight! A-yee-sha fight! Woman like a man, fight! Woman like a man fight!"

Musa was not amongst them though - Mama Sojojin confined him to rest and recovery in the medical tent away from the others.

Amina was hopeful that from the next day, training would include more than running. But all morning of the second day, the initiates were subjected to running.

Sometime around midday, she took a nature break. Upon emerging from the bushes, she found Mahmud waiting for her by the edge. He was smiling.

"I managed to steal away just to see you," he said with the gleeful look of a child with a carefully guarded secret.

Amina rushed to him and threw her arms around his neck, hugging him tight. She winced from hurt sustained in her knuckles while punching Musa the night before.

Mahmud pulled her away from him, so he could examine her blistered knuckles.

"Are you ok?"

Amina ignored the question. Her knuckles would heal. She smiled warmly at his tenderness, kissed him lightly on the cheek, and then planted a quick peck on his lips.

Mahmud's eyes twinkled. He leaned forward to kiss her again, but she withdrew and shook her index finger slowly at him.

"*Kai* Mahmud, respect yourself. This is no way to treat a decent girl. Besides, we must hurry back before we are missed." With that, she turned and ran back to the training ground. Mahmud stood rooted with a wistful smile on his face.

The routine for the rest of the second day was the same — running almost nonstop. The third day was no different and the fourth brought more of the same.

The only bright spots during the day for Amina were stolen nature break moments when she and Mahmud would meet in secret for a few stolen moments of kissing and hugging. She dared not risk meeting him in either of the large tents at night.

Amina soon began to dread her morning awakenings when she would hear the familiar brash voices of Madaki Zaki and other trainers ordering the initiates to rise and ready themselves for the day's training.

As Amina's adolescent body ached and faltered under the rigorous endurance training, she found herself cursing the day she asked her grandfather for permission to become a warrior.

The endurance training lasted for more days than Amina cared to count. The days quickly became a blur so much so that when she did realize that running up and down the hill had gotten mechanical and that her legs no longer felt like rubber or her chest like it would explode, her excitement did not return.

The running became something she did without little to no preparation. She began each run with a vision of her destination and seemingly did not think to stop until she completed her task.

She took fewer water breaks, ate rapidly, and stopped complaining altogether. It was a stark contrast from the early days when she would break down with exhaustion and suffer the lashes of the trainers' dried leather whips.

One morning, as she crouched and readied herself for the uphill run, shielding her eyes from the full glare of the sun, Madaki Zaki gripped her by the arm and held her back.

"Enough running."

Amina straightened up, her eyes like one who had just awakened from a trance. She turned to face her trainer and when he smiled at her with a slow nod of approval, she realized that she had successfully completed her first stage of training.

She looked around her.

There were quite a few other warrior initiates who had completed the first stage as well.

Mahmud was one of them.

Amina was pleased.

She closed her eyes, breathed in and savored the fresh morning breeze of the Harmattan season. She had not allowed herself the pleasure of nature's offerings for many training days. She had developed an uncanny intensity, an ability to shut out everything around her - her bruised, bleeding feet, the enduring pain, and the obstructive elements of dust and wind. She had learned to shut out everything that distracted from a singular purpose.

Madaki Zaki handed her the same metal sword and shield he had thrown down by her bed on her first day of training many days before. He took a few steps back from her and brandished a leather whip.

"Warriors! You who have successfully completed the endurance training will now be trained in the art of sword fighting and defense. To begin, each of you will spar with a trainer. Each trainer is armed with nothing but a whip. Each of you, on the other hand, has been provided a sword and shield. Hardly a fair match up. But we trainers are a benevolent group."

The trainers, standing in a row beside Madaki Zaki laughed aloud at his sarcasm.

Madaki Zaki continued. "Your task is to defend yourself with your shield and to attack with your sword when you sense an opportunity. You must do whatever is necessary to stop your trainer from defeating you. Do not show mercy and do not hesitate."

Madaki Zaki had hardly finished speaking when Amina sprang forward, hoping to catch him by surprise. She charged at him, her sword thrust forward, and her shield inadvertently lowered. She was the only one of all the promoted initiates that seized the initiative.

But it made no difference.

Madaki Zaki's instincts were sharp as a gazelle's feeding in open terrain. He moved swiftly to a side, evading her charge. As she surged past him, he struck her hard on the back with a clenched fist. His blow sent Amina tumbling to the dust, her sword flying in one direction and her shield in another.

She yelled out in pain as she landed on her chest. But she quickly recovered, spinning around and scrambling to her feet. She had assumed Madaki Zaki was unlikely to allow her time to recover and she was right. He was already standing over her, whip held high. But he refrained from landing it on her flesh.

"Excellent initiative Aisha. You have the instincts of a leader. But you must learn that defense is equally as important as attack. You left yourself completely exposed when you charged blindly at me. You must hold up your shield when you tactfully seek out an opportune time to strike your enemy."

Madaki Zaki took a few steps back and then called out. "Again! Come at me."

So began another monotonous routine for all the promoted initiates. For Amina, it turned out to be a miserable first day of combat training where she performed poorly in attack and defense.

She received instruction time and again from Madaki Zaki but was unable to balance her eagerness to improve with the patience required to learn.

She suffered lashes time and again. Although the whip was padded with rubber to prevent laceration, it hurt nonetheless. By the end of the day, Amina was miserable, angry, and certain she had had enough of it all. Her muscles ached, and her skin was sore. She wished she could strip it off like she would a piece of apparel.

As darkness began to set in and training for the day concluded, Amina motioned to Mahmud and excused herself for a nature break. Mahmud waited for a while and once others were distracted, actively engaged in packing up their gear, he headed for the bushes to join Amina.

"I don't want to be a warrior anymore," Amina blurted out. She felt like crying but forced back the tears, her voice quivering from the anger and physical strain she felt.

"Ok," Mahmud said and continued walking into the bushes, without even pausing to look at Amina.

Amina was stunned.

What had happened to the wonderful warrior initiate who was so fond of her? She had expected him to at least have a conversation with her, to perhaps comfort her, tell her this was the path all great warriors walked, or something like that.

But no, the idiot just kept on walking.

Overcome with rage, she searched the ground around her frantically, grabbed a small rock and hurled it at Mahmud's retreating figure.

He might as well have had eyes on the back of his head for he dodged the rock just in time.

He turned around to face Amina and burst out laughing.

'Not funny," Amina said, folding her arms, a deep frown on her face.

Mahmud walked back to where she stood. When he reached her, he placed his palms on her shoulders and locked his eyes with hers.

"Amina, the first and last thing you have said to me each time we are together is how much you have dreamed of becoming a warrior. You have told me how angry you were when your mother would not let you train.

You have told me how angry you were that training was reserved for men only. And, I have seen with my own eyes what you are capable of when threatened by someone twice your size."

Mahmud paused and smiled for his last words to register. Amina tried in vain to squash a smile.

"So, tell me - why, oh why, would I ever take you seriously when in a moment of exasperation, you say you are done?"

Amina reached out and hit him playfully.

"Come here, you idiot," she said, pulling him into a soft kiss on his lips.

♦♦♦

The days seemed to fly by after that day. Soon thirty days of training passed. During the last fifteen days, her training had evolved to sparring with other initiates.

Each day she was given a different sparring partner. Amina lost more sparring battles than she won. Each time she lost, the victor was surprised. Her opponents had expected her to win quite easily given the extraordinary ability she had demonstrated when fighting with Musa that first night.

Some suggested Amina faked the losses to appear more ordinary. But Amina did not fake the losses. She too had expected to win easily and initially only applied herself minimally to instruction.

But as she lost more than she won and grew frustrated with her losses, she was compelled to hunker down and learn the art of fighting just like all the other initiates. Though her losses frustrated her, she soon developed an appreciation for the lessons they provided.

On day thirty, Amina stood at the far end of the training valley. Her eyes were squeezed shut and her breath issued in measured spurts. She began each sparring battle oblivious of which warrior initiate would be her opponent.

In one hand, she clutched her metal sword which she had now mastered. In her other hand, she gripped her shield which she was still not quite adept at using, for she much preferred to attack than to defend.

Madaki Zaki and other trainers stood on the sideline of the valley floor, about the midpoint between Amina and her opponent. Beside Madaki Zaki, and, in a circle around the center of the valley floor, the rest of the initiates gathered like they always did for each spar.

They had been instructed to observe each battle and learn from the errors and expertise of each fighter.

"It is time!" Madaki Zaki declared the words that triggered the start of each contest.

Amina heard the battle cry before she felt the rumble of her charging opponent's feet. Her eyes flew open and she attempted to calm herself like she usually did.

Casting her feet wide astride for balance, she grasped her sword's embroidered handle with one hand and positioned the blade vertical to her face. Her other hand lifted her shield up to protect her chest.

She recognized the charging warrior and felt her heart skip a beat. It was Musa. Ever since Musa resumed training, Madaki Zaki had ensured he and Amina never directly crossed paths.

Why would Madaki Zaki have her spar with him now? He had to know that this spar would be tainted by his desire for vengeance.

Amina had little time to ponder the wisdom of Madaki Zaki's decision as Musa was upon her. The heavy blade of his sword landed hard on her shield as she raised it for protection and the impact sent her careening to the ground, her shield landing a few feet away from her.

Musa closed in on her quickly and soon stood over her, grinning, sword in hand.

Amina noticed he did not even carry a shield. *Arrogant fool!*

Musa stooped, cupped his hand around her chin and pulled her up, chin first. As her head came in line with his, he head-butted her as hard as he could.

Amina yelled in pain, feeling her world dim as her head crashed to the ground with blood gushing from her broken nose.

There was a loud wave of gasps from the shocked audience. There was mild chatter all around. Many questioned how it was that she was getting beaten by Musa whom she had defeated that first night.

"*Stand up! A-yee-sha, A-yee-sha fight! Woman like a man, fight!*" Musa mocked her with the now famed chant, his eyes glinting.

"You are no warrior. You are weak!"

Madaki Zaki looked on from the sideline. He had orchestrated this fight. He, like the initiates, expressed his opinion about the fight as well. He expressed his frustration to Ahmed.

"I am pleased with her commendable combat skills and what she has learned thus far. But I had hoped she would be untouchable by now."

Ahmed nodded in agreement, keenly watching the battle.

Musa lifted Amina and tossed her to the ground. As Madaki Zaki saw Amina fall backwards like a broken wooden doll with blood from her nose gushing like water from a creek, his eyes widened with alarm and he clenched his fists.

"She must not get hurt beyond what is expected from normal training. Habe Nohi would hold me accountable if does," he muttered.

For a moment all was still, and Amina appeared unresponsive on the ground. Madaki Zaki began rising to go to her aid when he observed a most bizarre occurrence that stopped him instantly, chilling the hairs on the back of his neck.

He could still see Amina's unresponsive body on the dusty ground. But now it looked to be more like her shadow lying crumpled on the ground.

It was as though Amina had split herself into shadow and body. Her shadow remained on the ground. But Amina's body had risen, sword positioned in hand.

Amina began fighting Musa with impressive skill, speed, and strength

Musa was caught off guard by Amina's sudden transformation and found himself backpedaling with his sword raised in frantic defense of each powerful blow she dealt.

He was losing control as she charged him down, forceful and relentless in her attack.

"This...this...cannot be happening, not again." Musa's eyes widened with shock and fear.

The sheer strength in Amina's blows was incredible!

Musa tried to catch her eyes. She appeared crazed with the force of her blows but in perfect control of her abilities.

Again, and again, she struck, moving rapidly forward in attack as he retreated in defense. She struck high and low in successive flashes with near impossible dexterity. He struggled to counter her blows, struggled to anticipate where she might hit next.

Finally, his strength and balance failed. He stumbled, collapsing onto his backside and losing control of his sword which clattered to the ground beside him.

Amina took swift advantage of his fall and closed in on him. She stuck the tip of her sword to his chin and pushed hard until blood spurted.

Loud cheering erupted from the sideline and the chanting began.

"A-yee-sha fight! Woman like a man fight! A-yee-sha fight! Woman like a man fight!"

"Who is the weak one now?" Amina mocked, her chest heaving.

Musa looked up at her, eyes engorged with fear. "Please," he muttered. "I was overcome by anger. Show mercy."

Amina held her sword in place for a moment, her fierce eyes like daggers pointed at his.

Madaki Zaki remained crouched at the sideline, observing it all in awe. He had been halfway between rising and squatting when Amina's turnaround began. He looked back to the floor where he had observed the miraculous separation of shadow and body. There was nothing there. He returned his focus to Amina.

Amina inhaled a few times to calm herself. Then she began to retreat from Musa, slowly, her eyes not leaving him for even a blink. When she felt she had given him enough room, she stopped and declared in a loud voice.

"Kneel and surrender Musa."

Musa, still reeling from the force of her attack, lifted himself to his knees and bowed his head. He was done fighting her.

Amina raised her sword and touched the back of Musa's head with its tip. Then she lifted her eyes and looked around the stunned audience. The silence was thick as fog on an early morning.

Amina felt empowered. The way they all looked at her made her feel like she ought to say something a leader would say. She raised her voice and the words came forth.

"Hear me everyone. Today, we spar but tomorrow we may be called upon to fight for Zazzau. It is important that we never let personal grievances cloud our judgment. If we desire to live in peace, then we must learn to fight as one. Warriors must learn to live and die together as one."

Mahmud, who was standing barely a few feet away from Madaki Zaki, dropped to his knees, clasped his palms together and rested his forehead on his clasped palms. He repeated her words. "Warriors live and die together."

Initiates beside Mahmud followed suit one after the other until the entire initiate class was kneeling in reverence. It was clear to all who had observed the fight that something extraordinary had just occurred.

Amina was taken aback by this development, this open show of allegiance. She welcomed it, relishing the exhilaration that it inspired within her. She declared again in a loud voice, and the warriors chorused in response, "warriors live and die together."

The crowd erupted in thunderous applause and all initiates and trainers poured onto the training valley to congratulate Amina. Madaki Zaki was about to go join them when a voice spoke behind him.

"Perhaps she is now ready!" The voice was Mai Sihiri's.

Madaki Zaki turned, his eyes wide with shock, to see the wiry old body of Mai Sihiri leaning on his rugged wooden staff. The sorcerer was enthused, smiling with his broken teeth in full glare. Madaki Zaki had not heard Mai Sihiri come up behind him.

"Was this your magic at work?" Madaki Zaki asked Mai Sihiri pointedly.

"Not at all, Madaki Zaki. This was Amina discovering her warrior spirit. I simply gave her spirit a little push and once she found it, she found abilities our ancestors had buried deep within her spirit long before she was even conceived. These are abilities your training has helped harness."

Madaki Zaki swung his head back to the training valley and took in the scene. There was Amina, standing tall with sword and shield in hand as her entire class celebrated her.

"Perhaps she is indeed ready," he said.

"Does she have the ability to summon her warrior spirit all by herself now?" Madaki Zaki turned to face Mai Sihiri. But the wiry old man was gone.

Madaki Zaki looked around but Mai Sihiri was nowhere around.

Madaki Zaki smiled to himself. "Perhaps the wiry old sorcerer was never physically here."

CHAPTER TWENTY-ONE

The Plot Thickens

*Unchecked ambition is a wild fire that
consumes everything in its path*

I T WAS LATE EVENING in Zazzau. Delicious aromas wafted from clay cooking pots outside family huts across the village. Fatigued men hurried home from a long day's work on farms and textile markets.

The village bustled with activity as market dealings were hastily concluded and children hastened to finish street games knowing that their mothers would soon summon them home for family dinner.

Nikitau weaved his way through the bustling activity, blending in as one of those hurrying home to relax, his face concealed behind a heavy turban for additional disguise.

He was headed to his most trusted aide, Mutuwa Dole. He had opted to visit Mutuwa Dole in his own hut as he always did when the matter at hand demanded utmost secrecy.

Mutuwa Dole was enjoying a hearty meal of *tuwo shinkafa da miya kuka* in his sparsely furnished hut when he heard the familiar knock of his master: a tap, two knocks and another tap on his wooden door.

He ushered Nikitau in and the two men exchanged customary salutations. Once pleasantries were concluded, Mutuwa Dole pushed his unfinished dinner aside and attended fully to his master.

"So, what brings my master to my humble dwelling?" he asked. He felt both excitement and trepidation. Such a visit usually meant a mission fraught with risk and danger but also a promise of great reward.

"I trust you are alone at home as usual?" Nikitau asked, looking around the empty hut and back to Mutuwa Dole for confirmation.

Mutuwa Dole nodded. "It is as you have said, my master."

"Very good." Nikitau smiled and stretched his folded legs, leaning backwards on the wooden stool upon which he sat. He rested his back on the mud wall of Mutuwa Dole's hut and allowed his eyes to roam from his trusted aide's face to the ugly scar on his hand.

"You paid quite the price to gain the trust and confidence of Etsu Tsudi," Nikitau said, displaying no gratitude for the hurt Mutuwa Dole had endured.

Mutuwa Dole followed his master's gaze to the scar on his hand. He had replayed that incident time and again in his mind. Etsu Tsudi was a vile, evil man. The memory of his visit sent a shudder down Mutuwa Dole's spine.

"Yes, indeed my master. But I would do it again for you if I had to." Mutuwa Dole spoke the loyal words he felt obliged to say without pausing to think. He regretted the words almost immediately.

"Good!" Nikitau said, leaning forward and pressing on his rotund belly so that he could speak as directly to Mutuwa Dole as he could.

"I need you to make another trip to Etsu Tsudi. This time it is a matter of even greater urgency and of course, secrecy."

Mutuwa Dole felt certain his heart stopped. Memories of his last visit flooded his mind and he felt an overwhelming urge to plead, to beg that he be spared another visit to hell.

But he bit his tongue. Did he really have a choice?

Nikitau leaned forward still, his voice shrinking to a whisper. "You are to convey a very important message to the Etsu, a message you must protect more dearly than your own life."

He paused to observe Mutuwa Dole who now looked pensive like one confronted by a vicious viper.

"What is the matter Mutuwa Dole? Has your dinner made you ill?"

Mutuwa Dole tried to feign calmness. It would have been easier to crack palm kernels with his buttocks. So, he grabbed the excuse afforded him.

"Perhaps that is the case my master. Please go ahead. My ears are fully inclined to your bidding. I will prepare myself a mix of soothing herbs once you have departed and will get some rest. It is nothing."

Nikitau observed Mutuwa Dole curiously for a moment then continued, accepting his dubious excuse.

"In five days, we will celebrate the Sojojin Kara. This promises to be a special one as Amina, my daughter, is to be honored as the first female warrior of our beloved Zazzau.

The celebratory atmosphere will provide a useful distraction and the element of surprise is critical if my plan is to succeed. Furthermore, I hear rumors that the Etsu has enlarged his warrior ranks more than tenfold and that almost all Nupeland now swears allegiance to him.

If this is true, and he attacks with the full complement of his warriors, he is certain to succeed this time. You are to inform him about this opportune time to attack. Tell him that I, Nikitau, remain his loyal servant, ready now and forever to lead the people of Zazzau in service to him."

Mutuwa Dole nodded, forcing a smile. He cleared his throat to dispel his fear.

"I shall do exactly as you have requested my master. You are indeed wise and I'm certain the Etsu will see the wisdom of your suggestion. I look forward to the future of Zazzau under your leadership."

Nikitau reached into his inner robe and produced several gold coins as payment for Mutuwa Dole's services. Mutuwa Dole smiled greedily. He was excited about the prospect of his master's elevation to Habe. This would mean a significant elevation and prosperity for him as well.

CHAPTER TWENTY-TWO

Amina Comes of Age

Reason and Desire may co-exist as equals for a little while. But in time, one must prevail

"I CAN SCARCELY BELIEVE tomorrow is our Sojojin Kara; the day we officially become Zazzau warriors," Amina said to Mahmud with a broad, enthusiastic smile.

The two were relaxing on an enclosed grassy plain hidden by an assemblage of short bounteous trees. This plain was close to where Zazzau's main stream, Kubanni, merged with the larger River Kaduna.

The grassy plain was a serene area enchanted with the river in front and a backdrop of short trees surrounding. The air felt just right - cool and breezy.

Amina stumbled upon this spot a long time ago during one of her childish adventures and she had made a habit of returning to it to play, and more recently for serenity.

Now, on the eve of their formal admission into the Sojojin Zazzau, Amina had invited Mahmud to this favored spot to reflect upon their achievement.

Mahmud, seated next to Amina on the grassy plain, held her eyes for a moment. He nodded in silent agreement. He looked around him with a satisfied smile. Except for the occasional ripple, the Kubanni stream was largely calm, snaking its way unperturbed towards its parent river.

Mahmud returned his attention to Amina who was looking straight ahead, appreciating the gentle flow of the river. He admired her long face, her smooth brown skin, her full lips.

Amina was lost in her thoughts, wondering what life would be like after the Sojojin Kara. She had visited Mai Sihiri once training was over, eager for insight as to what the ancestors had in store for her.

Mai Sihiri had shared with her that she was special and destined for greatness. The ancestors would use her in wondrous ways. But his flowery words were devoid of the specifics she sought, and she had left his dwelling feeling like a hapless thirsty soul teased by mirages in a scorching desert.

Amina sensed Mahmud's eyes on her but purposely paid him no attention as she wondered about her future. She had grown fond of him and admired the considerable skill he had demonstrated during their training.

But she was also wary of allowing herself to develop deep feelings for any boy or man. She would never allow herself to be ruled by any male. She was convinced that the only way to guard her heart was to never lose control.

"Amina," Mahmud began. "I am still in awe of what you did in the training valley. How did you suddenly conjure up the speed and skill to defeat Musa during the final battle?"

Amina smiled and fluttered her eyelashes, looking down at her purple loin cloth. She slowly caressed a partially exposed thigh. She was aware of the effect she had on him and she enjoyed the tease. She tilted her head towards him.

"If I tell you, you will owe me."

Amina felt empowered but also intrigued by the boldness she felt when in control. She had initially only intended that she and Mahmud would sit and observe the beautiful landscape together.

But now, she saw an opportunity to tease him and exert control. It excited her.

Amina knew it was frowned upon for a girl to display any kind of affection for a male in Zazzau. Rather, the traditional way was for the interested male to express his interest to the girl's father and obtain permission to spend time with her. She was excited by the idea of being forward with Mahmud and charming him into bucking tradition.

Mahmud was happy to play along, his excitement mounting.

"Ok, my princess. What would it cost me?"

Amina suddenly leaned forward and pressed her lips on his. When she withdrew from the kiss, she whispered.

"Loyalty, Mahmud. If you want anything to do with me, you must promise loyalty."

As Amina withdrew from the kiss, she could see the longing burning in Mahmud's eyes. He was one season older than her, but she could tell from the look in his eyes that he had never laid with a woman.

Amina had never laid with a man either. But she did not feel shy or inexperienced. She felt empowered by being so forward with Mahmud. No girl in Zazzau would be this forward - she felt excited to do whatever she pleased.

He leaned forward to kiss her again, but she drew back.

"Err, loyalty?" Amina said with one raised eyebrow.

Mahmud nodded and attempted to kiss Amina again but this time she leapt to her feet and ran away, laughing.

"Now you must catch me first," she called out to him.

Mahmud groaned in frustration but found his feet. He chased after Amina's limber figure as fast as his legs could carry him.

CHAPTER TWENTY-THREE

The Last Straw

One must never complain about what one allows

THAT EVENING, NIKITAU WAS seated on his favorite stool in front of his lower hut, waiting upon his heavily pregnant wife to bring him dinner.

"Is the food not ready?" he called out. "Or am I to die of starvation?"

Inside princess Bakwa's hut, two servants scuttled around like scared mice, fixing their master a bowl of boiled yams and freshly peppered palm oil.

Princess Bakwa sat nearby on a small bench waiting for the servants to lay out the food on a tray which she would take to her demanding husband outside. She was tired and extremely irritable. Her feet were swollen and hurt badly. Her protruding stomach felt heavy like a sack of potatoes.

She would need assistance from the servants to stand so she could take the food outside. Her eyes filled with tears, but she quickly blinked them away and wiped her cheeks, so the servants would not see. She began adjusting her position, spreading her legs wide apart and easing closer to the edge of the bench so she could slowly push herself to stand with assistance from the servants.

Nikitau had his Burukutu gourd in his hand as usual. He took a quick swig and cursed under his breath as he lowered it from his lips. He had tried to make his wife's pregnancy as tough as he could, hoping that she might lose the baby.

But so far, she had remained pregnant. The damned baby was determined to survive. He was determined that neither Princess Bakwa nor any of her offspring would rule Zazzau. Not while he was alive anyway.

As Nikitau sat brooding the imminent arrival of an unwanted heir, Amina came bouncing through the open front gate. She had a song on her lips, a wide smile on her face and a spring in her step like a butterfly dancing on a bevy of blossoming flowers.

Nikitau glared at her, his temper flaring.

"Shut up!" he thundered, leaping off his stool and shaking his finger at her. His loosely wrapped loincloth almost slipped off his waist as he sprang to his feet, his features darkening like moody clouds on a stormy night. He had found an outlet for his anger and was prepared to fully unleash.

"Where have you been all day, young girl? Why have you not been home attending to your pregnant mother?"

Amina stopped cold in her tracks. Her hand clasped the blunt end of her sheathed sword which she now carried with her wherever she went. She stared at her father, her eyes narrowing. She was poised like a tiger ready to pounce.

Nikitau faced off with his daughter for a moment frozen in time. They stood like two predators primed for battle. Nikitau grew even more vexed that Amina was squaring her shoulders to him in a disrespectful manner.

But he also felt a tinge of fear.

He had heard the stories of Amina's sparring conquest during her training - the entire village had learned of her prowess. With each retelling, the story had been exaggerated. If what was rumored was even remotely true, then she was indeed favored by the ancestors.

Nikitau would, in times past, slap her hard for showing him such disrespect. But now he hesitated, searching her defiant eyes and eyeing the sword she gripped tightly at its base. He was uncertain as to how she might react if he acted on his impulse to strike her. She was now a warrior, not his helpless daughter anymore.

At that moment, Princess Bakwa waddled out of her hut carefully holding a round metal tray with food on it. Behind her, the two servants who had assisted with preparing the meal followed, each with a firm hand on Princess Bakwa's back, supporting her as best they could.

The tension evaporated like a puff of smoke once the food arrived. Nikitau licked his lips and hastily sat down to eat. Amina observed her mother's superhuman effort to set the clay bowl of boiled yams before her husband, straining to reach over her protruding stomach as she did so. She rushed to her mother's side and assisted her.

Nikitau seemed incognizant of the difficulty with which his wife served him. He gulped his food like a gluttonous dog and was too engrossed in his food to see Amina eye him with a look of disgust or hear her mutter quietly to herself.

"I will surely put an end to this maltreatment of my mother, one way or another."

CHAPTER TWENTY-FOUR

Sojojin Kara

The end of a tunnel is as bright as its beginning. The light makes it easier to forget the darkness in the middle

THE TALKING DRUMBEATS SOUNDED slow and quiet at first in the Zazzau valley plain. A large area of the training ground was fenced off on all sides by giant ceramic and porcelain vases; each brimming with tall beautiful flowers.

On each side of the fenced perimeter, an opening was permitted. Each opening was manned by two large Sojojin Zazzau warriors standing tall and statuesque with long, curved, open-mouthed horns between their lips. As the drums picked up pace, the warriors blasted their curved horns, rendering powerful sounds akin to alpha wolves calling to their packs.

Outside the fenced area of the training ground, the entire Zazzau village had gathered on all sides to celebrate the Sojojin Kara and witness the induction of the one hundred new initiates.

On every side of the fenced area, behind the thronging crowd of villagers, a battalion of Zazzau warriors five thousand strong was gathered - some on horseback and some on foot. As was customary, the entire Sojojin Zazzau was assembled to welcome the new warriors into their ranks.

Within the fenced area, festivities were in full swing. The drums sounded louder and happier and the horns trumpeted in harmony to the drumbeat. Male and female acrobat dancers attired with beads, bright colored peacock feathers and fastened loincloths around their groins, gyrated and flipped across the valley plain.

The one hundred initiates were assembled on the valley plain in orderly rows, awaiting the formal induction ceremony. They stooped respectfully, each on one knee with head bowed before Habe Nohi's throne.

Habe Nohi sat on his throne in a resplendent white babban rigga. Beside him, members of the royal household were seated on elongated wooden benches.

Nikitau would, in times past, slap her hard for showing him such disrespect. But now he hesitated, searching her defiant eyes and eyeing the sword she gripped tightly at its base. He was uncertain as to how she might react if he acted on his impulse to strike her. She was now a warrior, not his helpless daughter anymore.

At that moment, Princess Bakwa waddled out of her hut carefully holding a round metal tray with food on it. Behind her, the two servants who had assisted with preparing the meal followed, each with a firm hand on Princess Bakwa's back, supporting her as best they could.

The tension evaporated like a puff of smoke once the food arrived. Nikitau licked his lips and hastily sat down to eat. Amina observed her mother's superhuman effort to set the clay bowl of boiled yams before her husband, straining to reach over her protruding stomach as she did so. She rushed to her mother's side and assisted her.

Nikitau seemed incognizant of the difficulty with which his wife served him. He gulped his food like a gluttonous dog and was too engrossed in his food to see Amina eye him with a look of disgust or hear her mutter quietly to herself.

"I will surely put an end to this maltreatment of my mother, one way or another."

CHAPTER TWENTY-FOUR

Sojojin Kara

The end of a tunnel is as bright as its beginning. The light makes it easier to forget the darkness in the middle

THE TALKING DRUMBEATS SOUNDED slow and quiet at first in the Zazzau valley plain. A large area of the training ground was fenced off on all sides by giant ceramic and porcelain vases; each brimming with tall beautiful flowers.

On each side of the fenced perimeter, an opening was permitted. Each opening was manned by two large Sojojin Zazzau warriors standing tall and statuesque with long, curved, open-mouthed horns between their lips. As the drums picked up pace, the warriors blasted their curved horns, rendering powerful sounds akin to alpha wolves calling to their packs.

Outside the fenced area of the training ground, the entire Zazzau village had gathered on all sides to celebrate the Sojojin Kara and witness the induction of the one hundred new initiates.

On every side of the fenced area, behind the thronging crowd of villagers, a battalion of Zazzau warriors five thousand strong was gathered - some on horseback and some on foot. As was customary, the entire Sojojin Zazzau was assembled to welcome the new warriors into their ranks.

Within the fenced area, festivities were in full swing. The drums sounded louder and happier and the horns trumpeted in harmony to the drumbeat. Male and female acrobat dancers attired with beads, bright colored peacock feathers and fastened loincloths around their groins, gyrated and flipped across the valley plain.

The one hundred initiates were assembled on the valley plain in orderly rows, awaiting the formal induction ceremony. They stooped respectfully, each on one knee with head bowed before Habe Nohi's throne.

Habe Nohi sat on his throne in a resplendent white babban rigga. Beside him, members of the royal household were seated on elongated wooden benches.

After an extended period of celebration, the drumming subsided, and the dancers exited the valley plain.

Madaki Zaki trotted on horseback through a parted crowd of villagers until he had come into the valley plain. He bowed low atop his horse to Habe Nohi who flashed a satisfied smile and raised his hand in acknowledgment. Madaki Zaki turned his horse to face the initiates and proudly declared.

"Brave warrior initiates of our beloved ancestral land. You have proved yourselves worthy of joining the coveted ranks of the Sojojin Zazzau. You have demonstrated loyalty to his highness; Habe Nohi and to our entire village. Today, you will be duly rewarded for your loyalty."

Madaki Zaki paused to allow his words register. The silence was deafening. Everyone knew what would occur next. The warrior who had trained with the utmost distinction would be recognized publicly before all the others were duly initiated. There was no doubt as to who merited the coveted recognition.

Madaki Zaki continued, declaring in a loud voice. "Let the one who is known as Aisha amongst you, rise and step forward."

Amina, positioned in the center of the first row of initiates, rose with her head bowed out of respect to the Habe and to

Madaki Zaki. She kept her right hand on her chest as a sign of loyalty. With her left hand, she clasped the blunt end of her sheathed sword in battle-ready position.

As Amina stepped forward, the audience erupted in rapturous applause and whistles of approval and celebration. The applause continued long after she had reached Madaki Zaki's horse. When the applause subsided, Madaki Zaki alighted from his horse, and spoke again.

"Turn around and show yourself to the village."

Amina did as she was told, raising her head and looking across the vast population that had come to witness the day. Her heart was beating so fast, she felt it might leap out of her mouth.

She had been informed the prior night that this honor would be bestowed upon her. But it had not quite sunk in until this moment. She had witnessed many warrior initiates being honored in this manner and had never thought it possible that she would even train as a warrior, much less be recognized as the most distinguished warrior initiate.

"All, I present to you, Amina, your princess, granddaughter of his royal highness, Habe Nohi."

A loud gasp swept across the crowd and across her fellow initiates. Many of the kneeling initiates broke protocol and looked up at her dumbfounded. The one they had assumed was a commoner named Aisha was the royal Princess Amina?

Madaki Zaki laughed and continued.

"Yes, indeed my people. This calls for a double recognition. Royalty shed the comforts and pleasures of the palace to train like a commoner and has come out on top. In our daughter Amina, we have found a true leader, one who has chosen to lead her initiate class by example."

Princess Bakwa, seated on the right of her father, smiled proudly and rubbed her protruding belly as she heard the accolades bestowed upon her daughter.

Nikitau was seated on the opposite side of Habe Nohi. He glanced to his right a few feet from where he sat and raised his eyes at Mutuwa Dole who stood with the rest of the palace servants.

Mutuwa Dole nodded calmly to his master. Nikitau smiled, satisfied, and refocused on the ceremony.

CHAPTER TWENTY-FIVE

Etsu Tsudi Strikes Again

It is a grave error to let one's guard down, to assume one has mastered the face of terror

THERE WAS ONE VILLAGER who had stayed away from the festivities. Mai Sihiri had stayed in his cave, burdened by a gnawing desire to consult the ancestors. He sat on the bare earth by a burning fire, rocking himself, and chanting incantations nonstop, beseeching the ancestors to reveal to him why he felt so burdened.

Now and again, he would toss a few tiny bird skulls into the fire and watch it sizzle, the flames seemingly annoyed by his interference. He was so engrossed in incantation that he failed to realize when he slipped into a trance.

Suddenly, he was spiritually transported to the valley plain where the Sojojin Kara ceremony was occurring. He saw everything clear as though he were there in person.

He saw Habe Nohi honoring Amina with a beautiful wrist bracelet laced with small, dazzling diamonds. He saw Madaki Zaki standing beside the Habe, radiating with enthusiasm. He saw the crowd of villagers going wild with joy, applauding Amina's achievement. He saw the dancers in a corner of the valley plain, readying themselves to take the stage once the honor and initiation ceremony was complete.

But, like stormy clouds suddenly arresting a tranquil sky, the joyous picture before Mai Sihiri vanished in an instant. That which he now beheld struck fear into his heart with the force of a dagger.

He cried out in terror. But no one heard him. For though he bellowed as loudly as he could, his voice sounded small and mellow because he was physically far away from his partying kinsmen.

It sounded loud and rough like thunder's angry growl - a multitude of charging horse hooves rumbling as if the earth was shifting under all Zazzau.

It happened fast, too fast for many to comprehend what was about to happen before it did. The Nupe warriors that suddenly poured down the valley peaks and into the valley plain on foot and horseback numbered in their tens of thousands, seemingly appearing like apparitions out of thin air.

The Nupe warriors charged towards the celebration center like ants streaming down an anthill on a single-minded mission without care or concern for safety or survival.

The blessings of Majiya, the Nupe medicine man rang loud in the charging warriors' ears as the victory charms and amulets he had provided them jiggled on their waists, arms and ankles.

These warriors that descended on the valley were led by Mokwa and by Etsu Tsudi himself. Etsu Tsudi wielded a sharp machete, his face hidden behind his macabre mask with horns which spiraled skywards and a protruding nose, sharp and extended like a bird's beak.

Mokwa rode by his ambitious leader's side, his eyes reddened, and battle hardened by the sun-dried herbs he had smoked to boost his confidence.

Chaos ensued, and confusion reigned.

Zazzau villagers scattered, fleeing from the attackers like bees abandoning a besieged hive. Wails of terror replaced the joyful drumbeats that had sounded only moments ago.

Zazzau's warriors were caught flat footed and scrambled to react. But struck with dread and dysfunction, they faltered and floundered. They fell victim in droves to the machetes and spears of the invaders, and their bodies quickly mounted in bloodied heaps.

Madaki Zaki had mounted his horse and galloped towards Habe Nohi, urging the horror-struck Habe to climb on behind him and flee the ambush to safety.

But Habe Nohi, despite his shock, remained primarily concerned for his family, and for his people. Ignoring Madaki Zaki's desperate motions for him to mount the horse, he leapt off his throne, yelling instructions for Princess Bakwa to be protected.

As royal servants rushed to the princess, he desperately scanned the valley turned bloodbath ground for his granddaughter.

Amina, like everyone else in Zazzau was reeling from the shock of the ambush. She had precious little time to draw her sword before the first Nupe attackers were upon her.

Amina moved quickly, desperately defending herself against the initial onslaught. She struck down two fury-blinded Nupe warriors that had fancied her an easy picking and looked feverishly all around her at the developing horror and carnage.

Zazzau warriors were falling faster than she could comprehend. Decades of life and livelihood were being severed by blade, arrow and fire. Amina spotted some members of her warrior initiate group fighting. Her heart burned, and tears stung her eyes as she saw some of her group fall to the blade.

She looked around, searching for Mahmud. But she could not find him in the commotion. She saw Musa, fighting valiantly and considered going to aid him.

Suddenly, Nupe warriors were upon her again. She moved just in time, dodging an axe that had been targeted at her face. But the axe shaved her left shoulder which had been left exposed by her sudden dodge. Amina yelped in pain but was careful to retain a grip on her sword and shield.

Her eyes locked with the eyes of her attacker. He, seeing her injured and assuming she was vulnerable, lunged at her again, expecting to finish her off.

But Amina was ready for him this time. She raised her shield, feeling it reverberate as the force of his axe came down hard on it. His axe stuck in her shield and as he struggled to free it, Amina saw an opportunity for victory.

She released her shield. The sudden impact caused him to fall backwards and to the ground. His eyes widened in sheer terror as he realized he was defenseless with his back on the ground. Amina lunged at him, plunging her sword deep into his midsection and twisting it viciously until the cry on his lips faded and his eyes froze, lifeless like a stone statue.

Amina pulled her bloodied sword out from his stomach and retrieved her shield. She cast her eyes around her as far as she could see. Everywhere she looked, blood from fallen warriors and wounded horses colored the earth.

The Zazzau warriors who were still alive were fighting a losing battle. Their families, defenseless women and children, scuttled helplessly for refuge like trapped mice in glaring light.

Amina's heart ached from shock and anguish. She looked up to the skies and cried out to her ancestors for empowerment, for deliverance. But as she raised her tiring arm to battle yet another Nupe attacker, she felt no extraordinary ability or ancestral intervention. She realized that the ancestors would not come to her aid. If Zazzau did not surrender, the village would soon be nothing but a wistful memory.

Habe Nohi had continued to look around but was yet to spot Amina through all the mayhem. He heard some of the royal servants he had instructed to protect Princess Bakwa scream in pain as flaming enemy arrows pierced their backs.

Habe Nohi saw them drop to the ground like flies, their bodies set ablaze by the fire on the arrows. He heard Madaki Zaki again yelling as loud as he could, urging him to hasten to safety. Habe Nohi was not one to be indecisive but he felt drained of all willpower. This was too much.

He looked around wearily - his people were falling everywhere; warriors and villagers alike were being slaughtered. Helpless, weeping children were being mercilessly slaughtered as well. He had grabbed a machete ready to fight with his people. But now his shoulders dropped, and his hand dropped to his side. His machete clattered to the battle field.

He had to stop this madness before all of Zazzau was massacred. He looked up and around again, anxious to find his granddaughter. He still could not find her.

Habe Nohi felt a hand on his shoulder. He turned and came face to face with Madaki Zaki. Madaki Zaki was yelling something. But Habe Nohi could not hear him. He felt as though he was in a trance - a transient ghost amid the slaughter.

He looked behind him. The servants he had asked to protect princess Bakwa had formed a circular shield around her. All but three of them had dropped dead from poisoned arrows. It was only a matter of time before Princess Bakwa was fully exposed.

Suddenly Habe Nohi heard Madaki Zaki gasp. He felt the hand that had grabbed his shoulder loosen its grip. He turned with wide, alarmed eyes to face his supreme commander again.

But Madaki Zaki had sank to his knees, his eyes bulging with pain, an arrow lodged deep in his heart. Blood oozed out of the side of his mouth as he tried in vain to speak. He began to cough and gasp violently for air.

Habe Nohi reached out and caught the falling Madaki Zaki. He felt tears sting his eyes and he cried out in agony as his heart ripped in half. What had he done? Had he listened to Madaki Zaki, this might not have happened.

Habe Nohi laid Madaki Zaki's corpse on the ground as gently as he could and quickly sprang to his feet, swinging his hands high up to the sky in surrender. He had to end the slaughter now.

He yelled at the top of his grief-stricken voice.

"Stop this madness! Stop the killing! We surrender! It is over!"

But like a river overcome by a high tide, the conflict did not instantly abate. Through the deafening sounds of sorrow and agony from Zazzau villagers all around, Etsu Tsudi heard Habe Nohi's call for surrender. Recognizing his moment of victory, he signaled one of his warriors to sound the conflict cessation horn.

As the loud blare of the battle horn sounded, the Nupe invaders began to round up all Zazzau survivors, forcing them to gather in the plain that had only recently served as a bastion of their celebration.

The entire valley plain was now a carnage of death and destruction, littered with battered bodies and severed limbs that stretched wide across the horizon. There was wailing everywhere. Women and children were pushed and shoved. Those mourning the dead were separated from the remains of the loved ones they cradled.

Before long, the gathering of survivors was completed. A bloodied Amina stood with her mother, father, and grandfather before the remnant of Zazzau. It was a population cut to half the number that had begun the day.

Amina was perplexed. She had battled hard and expected the ancestors to empower her with supernatural ability as they had done in the past. They did not, and she was left dumbfounded as to why they had ignored her.

Why they had forsaken Zazzau in its time of need? Amina was heartbroken. She had lost Madaki Zaki. She had lost many others she knew that day. Some had even sacrificed their lives for her, believing it their duty to protect the Habe's granddaughter even if it meant losing their lives.

Now, standing helpless and dejected before her decimated kinsfolk, Amina cast her eyes downward and the tears streamed down her face. She could see Madaki Zaki's lifeless body only a few yards away. Why, why had the ancestors allowed this to happen?

Vultures and birds of prey had begun circling the sky above. The air was filled with the stench of death. Almost every part of the valley plain was strewn with human corpses and horse carcasses. Nupe spearmen inspected the valley, verifying the dead and killing off any injured persons they found who were more dead than alive.

Behind the spearmen, other Nupe warriors followed, torching the corpses and carcasses, leaving behind them a rising blaze of death and destruction.

Etsu Tsudi, with his mask off, dismounted from his horse and walked towards Habe Nohi.

"Kneel before me," he growled at the Zazzau remnant before him. His voice was guttural, and his eyes were red and unmerciful.

Habe Nohi knew it was useless to resist. He obeyed. His family followed. And, so did the rest of the broken village.
Etsu Nupe let out a hearty, self-satisfied laugh as the entire village knelt before him. Mokwa now stood behind him with tens of thousands of Nupe warriors alongside him.

Mokwa raised a chant. "*Bagbadoza!* Etsu Nupe is *Bagbadoza!*" The Nupe invaders chanted the words in unison. Mokwa repeated the chant three times and the invaders replied three times.

At the end of the third chant, Mokwa let out a victorious roar and began a dance, creating a small circumference around himself. He moved boisterously, jutting his head forward and back like a proud peacock. His eyes and body were intoxicated with the euphoria of victory. Again, the Nupe invaders followed suit, reveling in their victory, and gloating over the misfortune of their vanquished foes.

Etsu Nupe allowed the exultation to continue for a while, observing with pleasure the misery of his captives and the jubilation of his cohorts. Finally, he lifted his hand high to halt the celebrations.

"Nohi, stand up," he said.

Habe Nohi rose, his tired eyes locked with Etsu Tsudi's. Etsu Tsudi grinned, his eyes flooded with feral fervor, void of empathy and humanity.

He chewed on his lip, curiously observing Habe Nohi. He was curious to see if Habe Nohi would be overcome with a desperation to protect his people, and to protect the legacy of Zazzau even at the cost of his life. He grabbed Habe Nohi by the neck robes of his soiled babban rigga and whirled him around to face his kneeling people.

"Nohi, you will voluntarily relinquish control of Zazzau to me and whomever else I may appoint to rule your people on my behalf. You will do so now in a clear, loud voice that all of your people may hear you and voluntarily look to me as their ruler now and henceforth."

Habe Nohi remained silent. All that was left of Zazzau looked to him with misery, pain and despair on their faces. Habe Nohi tightened his lips and hardened his eyes before the sea of hopelessness that kneeled before him.

Etsu Tsudi began to laugh out loud. So, Habe Nohi was going make a feeble attempt to be noble after all.

"I will not repeat myself!" Etsu Tsudi exclaimed when his mirth subsided. His grave words hung ominously.

"Please Baba, do as he commands." Princess Bakwa pleaded.

"Please no, grandfather!" Amina countered, a look of defiance in her eyes. Etsu Tsudi looked from Habe Nohi's daughter who was now crying inconsolably to the defiant granddaughter and sneered.

"What a wonderful, conflicted family. It's a pity I don't have the time for you to decide as a family. You might not have noticed but your Habe here doesn't really have a choice."

"Baba, are you just going to kneel there and do nothing?" Amina asked, looking at Nikitau, who was cradling Princess Bakwa. His head bowed.

Etsu Tsudi looked at Nikitau and back to Amina, then burst out laughing. "Oh, I see. You don't know the full story young princess. Your father is going to be Habe. Why would he ever oppose me?"

Amina, eyes flashing, tried to lunge at Nikitau but was withheld by Etsu Tsudi's warriors.

"You are rotten, Baba! Rotten! How could you? How could you do this? Our ancestors will judge you a thousand-fold."

Princess Bakwa burst into fresh tears and pulled away from Nikitau who just glared into space with as much emotion as a rock. Habe Nohi cast a pitiful look at his wailing daughter and mouthed the words. "I am sorry."

Then, with a resolute demeanor, he cast his eyes upon his people and declared.

"My people, never forget who you are. We are the proud people of Zazzau, Hausa now and Hausa forever. We are descendants of Bayajidda and will never bow..."

The rest of his sentence died in his throat as the sharp end of Etsu Tsudi's blade pierced from his back and emerged through his chest. Chaos ensued as wailing erupted afresh. Some Zazzau warriors amongst the crowd, despite possessing no weapons, rushed blindly to the defense of their slain leader.

Ahmed, Madaki Zaki's assistant commander, who had been kneeling amongst the crowd, commanded that they restrain themselves. But in that moment of madness, his command went unheeded. Those who rushed blindly at their oppressors were instantly struck down.

Princess Bakwa began hollering and threw herself on her father's fallen, bleeding body.

Amina broke free from the warriors restraining her and lunged at Etsu Tsudi. She would surely have been stuck down by Mokwa but for Mahmud who thrust himself between her and Mokwa.

His courageous action proved fatal.

Mahmud's body fell to the ground, pierced in the stomach by Mokwa's sword. It was the last thing Amina saw as the world around her began to swirl.

Her face met the earth.

CHAPTER TWENTY-SIX

Captive

A battered body one can mend, but a broken spirit is lost forever

ARKNESS. THE DARKNESS WAS so overwhelming that it could have been mistaken for a powerful life form. To Amina, the darkness felt like an evil presence strangling her in a cold, cruel embrace. And that smell...what was that putrid smell? She knew what it was - human excrement, vomit, and urine.

Amina retched, then realizing that she was naked and shackled. She slouched to her right side. Her hands were suspended high, fettered at the wrists. Her legs were spread wide, fettered by her ankles. Her bare back, buttocks, and thighs were lacerated by the leather whip with which she had been repeatedly flogged.

Amina was weak and barely hanging on to consciousness. She was unaware that she had drifted in and out of consciousness for several days, oblivious to anything but pain and terror. She heard a muffled groan somewhere close by.

Her ears perked up. There it was again.

There was someone else in the room - someone else in a similar unfortunate state. Amina wondered who her fellow prisoner was.

"Amina."

The voice was weak and frail, but Amina recognized the voice instantly. She mustered what strength she could with tremendous effort and asked the questions that burned in her mind.

"Jamila, where are we? What happened in Zazzau? What happened to my mother?"

Her questions were met with silence first followed by a deep, anguished groan. Amina could hear Jamila shifting uncomfortably.

"Our Zazzau is no more, Amina, at least not the way we knew it." There was a pause as Jamila continued to gather strength to speak. She spoke haltingly, clearly exhausted and in significant pain.

"Zazzau has been taken as part of the Nupe empire. Princess Bakwa is alive, but she has been stripped of all royalty."

Another long pause.

"Amina, your father rules in your mother's stead as Habe. He was appointed by Etsu Tsudi. We, along with many other captives were brought here to Nupeland as slaves to serve at the Etsu's pleasure."

Amina felt tears roll down her cheeks as fear tightened its grip on her heart. She felt more helpless than she had ever felt. Even the news that her mother was still alive only offered minimal relief.

She realized that, with Nikitau on the throne, her mother would have been relegated to a mere servant before him. And Amina feared for the fate of her unborn sibling.

She recalled her slain grandfather and others she had lost - warriors, fellow initiates, Madaki Zaki, and Mahmud.

Oh Mahmud...he sacrificed himself to save her life.

She wept, and her body shook with heavy sobs. Was this the end then? How could this happen? In her mind and spirit, she called to the souls recently departed to join her ancestors. She silently petitioned for spiritual help to avenge them.

A small- statured elderly woman emerged through a small thatched door, allowing a brief glimpse of sunlight that momentarily blinded Amina. But just as suddenly as the light appeared, it was dark again as the woman shut the door behind her.

The woman carried a small oil lamp with a weak burning flame and a metal bucket. Amina tried to talk to the elderly woman. She was probably a slave. But the words failed her.

Amina was too weak to carry on any conversation. The woman cleaned as though she was forced to perfect it over time. She did not make eye contact with Amina nor did she attempt to converse.

Soon, Amina began to tremble anew in fear as she sensed the woman nearing completion of her task. What Jamila had shared terrified her. But the fear that now swept over her was different, more ominous. Something about this woman nearing the end of her cleaning routine was oddly familiar. But her body was too battered, and her mind was too burdened to permit any introspection.

Amina watched the elderly woman through weary eyes. Her body slouched even further, supported only by the hanging metal chains secured around her wrists.

The elderly woman concluded her task and then slowly approached Amina. She grabbed a wooden gourd of water from her wrapper and without warning, splashed water on Amina's face. She did the same to Jamila.

Amina gasped and squirmed in pain as the cool water swept over her bruised face. The water was both refreshing and shocking to her skin. She stuck her tongue out to lick whatever droplets she could that rolled down her forehead, cheeks and onto her lips.

As the woman turned to go, Amina again tried to speak to her. But again, words failed her. Soon the woman was gone. And the darkness settled over the room once more.

And then, it happened.

She felt hands, numerous hands grab her and begin groping her body from multiple directions. Amina yelled out in revulsion and agony. But in her weak state, her words barely sounded. They died in her throat.

Tears gushed from Amina's eyes and rolled down her face. She heard someone else screaming. Was that Jamila? It had to be. Or was it just her own spirit's distant cry? Perhaps her spirit, in anticipation of the cruelty, now cried so loudly that it penetrated the physical realm.

Amina felt what was happening. She felt it on her body and deep in her soul. But since she was physically restrained, and emotionally retired, she found herself utterly powerless.

She had struggled at first when her violators first attacked several days earlier. Now, she surrendered her body completely, opting to instead safeguard her mind in a distant, imagined place of solitude. These attacks had occurred multiple times over the past few days. Amina had fallen in and out of consciousness each time.

These violators were evil spirits determined to break her spirit. They were not merely Nupe warriors who appeared ubiquitous in the dark shadows of the prison. They were not mere men who waited patiently in the dark, eager to repeat the cycle authorized by the Etsu himself.

Amina could not bear to accept that men had succeeded in subjugating her in the most demeaning way possible. She once again called to her ancestors in her mind.

Would she die at the hands of these vile spirits? Why had the ancestors allowed men to humiliate her in this manner? Was she not Amina the Chosen? Did the ninety-nine other warrior initiates not praise her and celebrate her prowess, calling her a woman who was as capable as a man? Were the ancestors so cruel as to mock her by exalting her for a mere moment only to abandon her to such a wretched end?

Amina felt darkness closing in on her again. Reality had become a frailty which her mind struggled to retain control of. She felt herself slipping out of consciousness.

Amina welcomed the oblivion the darkness offered. Better to be wholly absent in mind while the evil spirits tormented her body. Let the demons have my body and the ancestors my spirit, she thought and closed her eyes – grateful for the bliss of nothingness that enveloped her.

♦♦♦

Amina found herself on the outskirts of Kamuku about two days walk from Zazzau. She had no memory of anything up to this point.

Kamuku was a vast forest surrounded by low vegetation lands and barren plains. This island-like forest was rich with an eclectic mix of tall grasses, all manner of trees, caves, and waterfalls over massive rock formations.

Amina rested for a while on a large boulder, eating wild berries and the sweet yellow pulp from the many locust bean trees. She felt some mild discomfort and her mind was an entirely blank slate. But her motivation was overflowing. She was determined to accomplish her mission. What was the mission though? Her mind drew a blank. She did not know. But she was certain she would discover it.

Amina slowly folded her legs, wincing as she pulled them up so that she could rest her chin on her knees. Her feet were sore from walking. Though she wore sandals for protection, she had still suffered cuts and bruises while probably maneuvering through wild grasses, and thorns. Beside her was a wood-carved bow, a leather quiver of poisoned arrows, and a leather satchel of survival essentials.

Amina glanced around her. In the distant horizon, the sun, now a giant yellow ball, was dipping against the backdrop of a clear amber sky. Although she was calm as a river under the spell of a blustering wind, she refused to panic outright. Deep within, she felt certain she would be alright.

Around Amina, there were thick, knee-length grasses, and a spread of tall, and short trees with branches networked high into the sky. Amina realized she needed to find a place to sleep while it was still twilight. She had a great vantage point from her elevated resting place and could see a mountainous area. She would head in that direction.

What was she to find in this forest? What was her mission? Again, she received nothing but an urging to proceed as powerful as the force of a violent wind. She swung her legs over the side of the boulder, spotted a safe landing spot, and jumped to the ground. As Amina moved through knee-length bushes towards the mountainous area, she became aware that the quiet forest was quickly livening with a cacophony of animal and insect chatter.

She could hear crickets, birds, and a plethora of sounds she couldn't recognize. There was the occasional howl, probably an

African wolf calling for his pack, and the sounds of laughing hyenas in response mocking the wolf's cry.

She walked for a while, caressed by a smooth evening breeze until she arrived at her destined mountainous area.

At the mouth of the mountainous area, the grasses were much shorter, and trees were conspicuously absent. Nature had cleared the area to allow a series of large rocky caverns that conjoined to form the extended mountains Amina had observed from a distance.

She was relieved to discover an accessible, wide-mouthed entrance to one of the conjoined caverns. The sun had almost completed its descent by now and much of what she could see was reduced to shadowy blurs.

As Amina contemplated, she felt a familiar tug at her heart. A strange brew of panic and excitement. Her mission was nigh! She also felt constrained.

What if there was a pack of wild animals living in the cavern? What if it was empty for now until the animals return to their habitat while she slept inside? These questions jarred her mind like an alarm horn sounded with an elephant's tusk.

Amina felt her muscles tense and her heart quickened its pace. She reached into the quiver on her back and pulled out a poison tipped arrow. She stretched it onto her bow and aimed straight ahead at the darkness in the cave.

She began to take cautious steps towards the cave entrance.

The evening breeze she had felt moments ago seemed to have expired, banished by the tension she now felt. Beads of sweat like tiny rain droplets began to form on her creased forehead, spilling into her eyes.

She wiped her forehead with the back of one palm and resumed her stealth poise. Her breath was measured, and her heart hurled itself against her chest.

Somehow, Amina felt in control. Her senses were heightened and harnessed for attack. She realized now just how much better prepared she was to defend herself. Madaki Zaki had trained her to ignore her weaknesses, and to reach deep down within for a strength that was beyond physical.

She looked down at a wooden talisman she wore around her neck. It was a small pendant carved in the shape of a lion. Mai Sihiri had gifted it to her when she went to visit him after she completed her warrior training. He had told her the ancestors had blessed her with the courage of a lion. The talisman should always remind her of that.

Amina breathed in deep and slow. Then, she exhaled long and hard. She moved on the tips of her toes, her eyes squinting and adjusting to the semi-darkness of the cavern.

The grassy dirt beneath her sandaled feet gave way to rocky ground as she stepped into the cave. The air in the cave was stale and the quiet.

Amina retained her cautious movement, her eyes darting in every direction possible. She was equipped with a flame wick, and some lamp oil in her satchel. She would need to light it, but not just yet. She hoped she could continue to take advantage of whatever little sunlight that remained.

Amina moved a bit farther into the cave. She saw that there were multiple tunnel openings within the cave. Each opening was already dark. The sunlight that remained outside was too weak to be of any use to her. She was faced with a critical decision - search in darkness or retreat to the outskirts of the cave and use the lingering sunlight to prepare herself effectively for the darkness within.

She paused for a moment, breathing heavy but measured breaths. Her eyes continued searching for movement of any sort in the darkening expanse before her. The decision was not a difficult one - it was already too dark inside. She took a cautious step backwards.

She heard a thunderous roar as a beast pounced from a stalking position atop the cavern about three head-lengths above her. Amina tripped on the jagged edge of a rock partially buried in the ground, avoiding instant mauling. She cut her heel on the rock as she fell.

Another roar reverberated across the vast bushy plain. Amina's fall had saved her from the claw of what she now saw was a vicious lion. The lion's claw scratched her upper right eyelid as she fell, drawing blood. She yelped in pain.

Amina landed on her back, and her bow clattered to the ground just behind her head. She rolled away from the lion. She grabbed her bow, quickly scrambling to her feet in adrenalin-powered paranoia.

The powerful beast snarled, and bared its teeth at her, poised to pounce again. Amina was shocked to see that this beast had a human face.

It was the face of Etsu Tsudi.

As she stared at the evil face before her, Amina felt like her heart freeze like ice in her chest. Her recent memories surfaced, evoking rage and sorrow hitherto buried deep within. She gnashed her teeth together, and tears filled her eyes as the memories of Zazzau's decimation battered her mind like a hailstorm.

Amina realized in a panic that she was armed with her bow but not her arrow. But the panic she felt was a transient emotion compared to the rage that suddenly powered her. She began to mutter a desperate prayer to her ancestors.

Surely, they would not abandon her again to be slaughtered like a common animal. Blood gushed from her butchered eyelid, almost blinding her right eye completely. But the adrenalin coursing through her now was so potent, she could barely feel the pain.

The beast growled, then seemed to burst into mocking raucous laughter. Etsu Tsudi was mocking her. She heard his words in her mind.

"You are nothing, Amina. You will always be nothing. You pleaded for mercy as I ravaged you in my prison, but your body did not deserve mercy. Your body was ready and eager to serve my every pleasure.

You are a weak and cowardly woman. My warriors tell me you squealed like a little girl as they took turns with you. You will never save your people. You, and your kin will forever bow to me, and forever obey my every command."

Amina had heard enough. She moved impulsively and was ready to pounce on the lion armed with nothing but a bow, and her bare hands.

But suddenly, something barricaded her way - a foggy barrier.

Amina attempted to thrust her hand through it but found to her surprise that the fog was solid as a wall. The fog had no physical outline, yet it was solid - a wondrous, solid fog.

Then she heard a bold, clear voice like thunder in the skies.

"Amina, you are a woman greater than any man. You have been praying for an endowment of power. But the power you seek already lies within you. Every lion cub is but a grown lion in waiting. A lion cub will only remain a cub so long as it perceives itself as merely a cub.

Amina, your ability must never be constrained by what you can see or understand. If you are to lead your people, then you must never be dominated by emotion or controlled by circumstance. You must live solely by the fortitude of will, and the certainty of choice.

You must ignore your human inhibitions, and believe above all else that we, your ancestors, are always with you, and are always working through you. When you fully embrace this undeniable truth, you will emerge as the one you are destined to be."

In the blink of an eye, the foggy wall disappeared as suddenly as it had appeared. Amina was stunned but had little time to process what had just occurred. She became aware that the lion was poised to attack her.

Through the corner of her eye, she sighted her arrow on the ground close to the entrance of the cavern. Its feathered blunt end was stained with blood from her wounded eye. She was almost certain the lion would reach her faster than she could reach the arrow. Her entire being was feverish with tension and fear. But the words spoken by the ancestral spirit now resounded loud in her spirit.

"If you are to lead your people, then you must never be dominated by emotion or controlled by circumstance."

Amina darted to grab the arrow. In her frenzied haste, she dropped her bow. The lion leapt towards her, its powerful paws and claws outstretched to inflict maximum damage. Amina felt her body slam the ground hard.

Suddenly, Amina felt something hit her hard on her right leg, and she screamed in agony. It was the weight of the lion's hind leg upon hers. Almost knocked unconscious by the excruciating pain, her right hand closed around the base of the arrow.

Buoyed by a renewed faith that her ancestors were always with her, she twisted swiftly on her backside, lifting the poisoned point of the arrow high in the direction of the animal's chest just as its menacing front paws were descending upon her.

She stabbed its chest.

There was a huge roar followed by a soft whine as the beast collapsed. Amina moved aside, narrowly dodging its limp crash to the floor. The lethal venom on the poisoned arrow was instant. Within mere moments, the life of the fearsome creature was extinguished.

Amina opened her eyes and blinked. There was a blurry light dangling before her. As her eyes focused on the bright spot in the darkness, she realized she had just regained consciousness.

Amina was still in the prison hut. The bright light before her emanated from an oil lamp. She squeezed her eyes and shook her head to focus.

She blinked again, attempting to master the reality of the moment. When her eyes finally accustomed to her surroundings, she saw the person holding the lamp. It was the small-statured elderly slave who had cleaned the prison hut early on.

She had been shaking Amina vigorously.

Amina sat up. She suddenly felt much stronger and was no longer shackled. She began to speak but the woman hushed her.

"You must leave now. Do it quickly before you are discovered."

Amina raised her eyebrows. She had a thousand questions.

The woman shoved her, a shove which barely moved Amina since she was at least twice the small woman's size.

"You must go now. I have prepared some fruits for you in a bag outside. You should take them with you to replenish your strength for the journey back to your homeland.

Look at the bodies on the ground around you. I poisoned the evil guards who assaulted you. It won't be long before new guards come to replace them. Leave now lest my assistance to you, and my sacrifice come to naught."

Amina looked down at the ground. Then, she looked around her, noticing the corpses of the Nupe men who had raped her. She began to rise. Her ancestors had somehow compelled this maidservant to orchestrate her rescue.

"But you will be tortured and killed for this," said Amina.

"They raped me too. I already lost my body and soul to many of these men. I am old now and if I die, so be it. I will die happy knowing that I played my little part to save someone else from the clutches of these evil men."

The woman paused and soberly motioned towards Jamila's body.

Sadly, I could not save your friend. See, they have killed her."

Amina turned in the direction of Jamila as the elderly slave held up the oil lamp for her to see. Jamila's body hung lifeless in shackles. Her corpse was stripped and bloodied.

Amina felt a retch but forced herself to contain it. Tears poured down her cheeks as she experienced flashbacks of innocuous play with Jamila - simpler times never to be relived. She struggled to calm her emotions and muttered under her breath.

"As long as I live, I swear I will avenge this wrong, and the many other wrongs done to me and my people. The evil that men have done to women shall be visited upon them one thousand-fold."

Amina was reluctant to abandon her best friend's corpse. But she realized she had no choice. She thanked and hugged the woman.

The maidservant handed her a wrapper and a leather loin cloth to cover her nakedness, and quietly ushered her out through a back door.

CHAPTER TWENTY-SEVEN

Aftermath

It is fortitude, not circumstance, that determines how the day will end

ZAZZAU HAD RETURNED TO normalcy. If it could be called that. Village routines had resumed. Men fished and farmed, women cooked and cleaned, and children chased one another on the dusty streets. Mass funerals had been conducted for the departed. All appeared normal again activity. But it was not so in spirit. The spirit of Zazzau was battered. A forlorn feeling pervaded the atmosphere and seemed to thicken with each passing day.

It was a sunny afternoon in Zazzau. The sun shone in dissonance with the cloudy mood in the village. Inside the palace, Habe Nikitau sat on his throne with two newly appointed advisers before him. Nikitau had disbanded all Habe Nohi's noble advisors. In time, he would find worthy advisors who would be loyal to him.

The two advisers before him were Mutuwa Dole, who was recently elevated to the position of Village Head, and Madaki Ahmed. Nikitau had ordered what remained of the Sojojin Zazzau to regroup under Ahmed, Madaki Zaki's assistant, once he swore allegiance to Nikitau as Habe, and Etsu Tsudi as the emperor of the vassal village of Zazzau.

"My esteemed Habe," Mutuwa Dole began. "May you live long, and rule Zazzau wisely. Our people say the one who does not recognize when it is time to plant will surely starve in the dry season.

My Habe, if it pleases you, I would like to suggest that now is the time to propose and negotiate the taxes we will be required to pay to our lord Etsu Tsudi.

At this moment, he is likely to regard us with compassion given our depleted numbers. I presume the Nupe clans are contributing more than enough to his coffers for now. But we must act now or risk losing our opportunity if we delay and allow him send us taxation terms first."

Habe Nikitau leaned back on his throne. Like his predecessor, he was dressed in traditional Habe attire - a flowing babban rigga with a turban adorning his head. He had neither considered nor contemplated what Etsu Tsudi might require of Zazzau in the aftermath of annexation. He had assumed he would happily comply with any requirements or orders handed to him.

However, Mutuwa Dole's words now gave Habe Nikitau pause as there was clearly wisdom in them. He had realized that critical decision making would be a main aspect of his duty as ruler of Zazzau. But this foreknowledge did nothing to assuage the discomfort he felt with making critical decisions.

Why should he care anyway? So long as he remained Habe of Zazzau, why should he care if some bad decisions were made? As a matter of fact, no critical decision would be ratified without the Etsu's consent anyway.

All Habe Nikitau was really interested in was enjoying the benefits of his newfound power. He had already informed Princess Bakwa that he intended to marry additional wives - younger wives that would bear him many sons. He had expected her to resist his decision and had been prepared to force her acceptance. But to his surprise, she offered no resistance at all. Perhaps it was because she was still grief-stricken.

Habe Nikitau decided that the right approach would be to appreciate Mutuwa Dole's counsel but dismiss any illusions of wisdom that his new Village Head might ascribe to himself.

As he leaned forward to speak, two palace guards suddenly entered the palace in a panic. They bowed hastily but waited, as was customary, to be permitted to share news.

Madaki Ahmed sprang to his feet.

"What is it? Why this disrespectful intrusion on an important village leadership meeting?"

The guards bowed again. The leader of the two spoke.

"Please forgive us, Madaki, our esteemed Habe, our..."

"Out with it!" Madaki Ahmed cut him short.

"It is Princess Amina, sir."

Habe Nikitau's eyes grew wide.

Mutuwa Dole sat up and asked, "Is Amina not in captivity with Etsu Tsudi?"

"What about Princess Amina? Madaki Ahmed demanded, addressing the lead guard. "You better start making sense."

"She is standing outside Zazzau's walls. She declares she is here to free Zazzau from the clutches of the evil Nupe empire. She swears she will challenge to the death the one who has sold our village to Etsu Tsudi, in exchange for the throne."

Silence ensued following delivery of the message. Mutuwa Dole felt his stomach doing flips. He had heard rumors of Amina's prowess.

Habe Nikitau laughed to feign confidence but his laugher sounded hollow. Inside, he was furious. How dare his own daughter challenge him to the death! Who was she to challenge his authority?

Habe Nikitau leapt off his throne and marched to the guard who had broken the unnerving news. He grabbed him by the neck of his dashiki and pulled his ear close.

"You take this message back to that little wretched daughter of mine. Tell her I accept her challenge, and that before the sun sets tonight, I will remind her that it is I who gave her life."

The guards hurriedly exited the palace to deliver the defiant response. Habe Nikitau began a quiet walk back to his throne, lost in thought.

He was afraid.

He had heard the rumors of Amina's prowess. Perhaps it would have been wiser to avoid confronting her. Perhaps he should have stalled and instead sent word to Etsu Tsudi.

He could have informed the Etsu that Amina had returned to Zazzau and requested assistance to recapture her. But Habe Nikitau did not want to wait for Etsu Tsudi. He felt insulted that his own daughter would challenge him openly like this. She needed to be punished for such insolence.

As Habe Nikitau reached his throne, he turned to Madaki Ahmed.

"Tell me, Madaki Ahmed. You were with Amina throughout her training. Is it true that she sometimes possesses ancestral powers?"

Madaki Ahmed had convinced himself that the rumors about Amina had been grossly exaggerated. Sure, he had witnessed a few occasions where she performed extraordinarily as a warrior. But every warrior had some good fights and bad ones. Were it certain that Amina possessed ancestral powers, then surely, she would not have allowed her beloved grandfather to be murdered.

"No, your highness. Those are baseless rumors that is the talk of idle, superstitious warriors."

Habe Nikitau smiled and breathed a sigh of relief. He sat comfortably on his throne and considered what to do about Amina.

"Madaki Ahmed. I have changed my mind regarding Amina's challenge. I have decided it is beneath me as Habe to engage a senseless little girl that thinks more highly of herself than she ought.

You will engage her in my stead. You go out there and teach her a lesson she will never forget. When she is ready to kiss my feet, and desperate to beg for my forgiveness, then bring her to me."

CHAPTER TWENTY-EIGHT

Making of a Queen

One who constantly observes his shadow shall never make progress

AMINA HAD BEEN TRANSFORMED. She was now a very different person from the young girl who had often stolen away from the village to watch the Sojojin Zazzau train. Her body was battered but her mind was clear and her resolve solid as steel. She had learned to focus on the power of her mind over the frailty of her body.

Getting back to Zazzau on her own had been challenging - she had hired herself out as a maidservant, scrubbing the deck floor on a rowboat in exchange for food and passage northwards on the River Niger from Nupeland. When the captain of the rowboat tried to force himself on her as payment for her passage, Amina killed him with his own dagger.

Now Amina stood, defiant and armed with the rowboat captain's dagger, outside the fence that formed a perimeter around the village of Zazzau.

Her skin bore every evidence of torture and suffering. But despite her poor physical condition, she had never felt stronger or more convinced that she was exactly where she was meant to be. Amina felt the sting of the burning sun on her blistered skin. But she didn't flinch. She was prepared to fight for the freedom of her people or die trying if her ancestors willed it.

She gritted her teeth and called out louder for her father to emerge, daring him or anyone in the village to accept her challenge. She declared that Zazzau could never be held captive for long. She encouraged all who could hear her to recall that her dying grandfather had urged them to never give up, never to accept tyranny as inevitable or permanent.

Amina was still yelling out defiant words when the large metal gates of the village opened.

Madaki Ahmed emerged. He looked up at the archers high up on sentry posts behind him, and held up his hand, indicating that they not shoot unless he commanded them to. Satisfied that they understood his command, he unsheathed his sword and advanced toward Amina, shield held chest high.

"Princess Amina, *menene wannan?* This is madness," he said.

Amina coughed and spat on the ground.

"No, what is madness is how you and Baba have surrendered your manhood to the Nupe dogs."

Just then, there was a loud shout from a woman who had suddenly emerged from the gates and attempted to run towards Amina. She was apprehended by two guards who had emerged chasing her. As she grappled with the powerful guards, she yelled desperately to Amina.

"Amina, please, I beg you my daughter, run from here at once! Your father has gone mad. I beg you, flee while you can."

Amina feared for her mother's safety and felt the urge to go free her from the clutches of the foolish guards that restrained her. But she reined in her emotions. She needed to remain focused on her mission.

She addressed Madaki Ahmed.

"Tell those idiots to do my mother no harm."

"Why don't you surrender so I can ensure no harm comes to your mother? No one needs to get hurt Amina. You are one of us. We can discuss this. I am certain we can work something out with your father, the new Habe."

She looked from him to her mother who was being forced back into the village behind the fence.

"So, you want to bargain for my mother's life now? Listen Madaki Ahmed...it is Madaki now, isn't it?"

Madaki Ahmed nodded.

Amina continued.

"I realize you are a warrior and you are only doing your duty to the so called new Habe of Zazzau. So, I will give you this one chance to save yourself.

Step aside. Go back into our village and ask my father to stop being a coward. Ask him to come out here and accept my challenge. So long as he falsely sits on the throne, our people can never be free. You do want our people to be free, don't you?"

Madaki Ahmed squirmed, offended by her. This was, after all, Amina - a girl whom he had helped train not too long ago. He tightened his grip on his sword.

"How dare you threaten me? This silly conversation has gone on for too long. You are still only a child, and a girl at that.

Stop this nonsense. You will do well to get into the village, and bow down to your father, our new Habe. You will do it now!"

Amina narrowed her eyes at him as rage surged through her. But she refused to surrender to its force.

Rather, she took a deep breath and breathed out very slowly, controlling her emotion and harnessing the fire of her vexation. She imagined herself striking Madaki Ahmed, taking a calculated action against him.

She imagined herself in control. She saw herself killing him for a justifiable cause - he had allowed his duty as a Zazzau warrior to blind him to what was truly important: the freedom of Zazzau.

When Amina moved, her action was sudden, swift, and precise. She leapt high, and charged towards Madaki Ahmed, dagger outstretched.

Madaki Ahmed was a skillful fighter. He quickly veered away from the direction of her incoming dagger. But Amina had somehow managed to withhold herself from completing her lunge towards him.

She pulled her hand back mid attack and turned midair towards the direction to which he had veered. Madaki Ahmed's eyes widened. He yelled in terror and tried to somehow adjust his bearings again while still executing his initial move. But it was impossible to move that quickly. Amina drove the dagger deep into his chest.

Amina landed, with her back to Madaki Ahmed, in a squat position a few feet away from where she had stabbed him. She spun around and rose, recovering her alert stance.

Madaki Ahmed tried to speak as he clutched his stabbed chest and blood colored his hands. His lips quivered, and his eyes bulged in shock as he silently mouthed her name.

Amina stared at his expiring body through steely eyes. "Call me a child. Call me just a girl. It matters not what you call me. It matters what I can do."

Madaki Ahmed collapsed to the floor in a cloud of dust.

Amina walked over to her fallen foe. When she reached him, she knelt beside him, and silently prayed that the ancestors would welcome his spirit. Then she reached over his face, and flipped his eyelids shut.

She rose to full stance and stretched her arms out until she stood like a cross, dagger in her right hand. She yelled at the top of her voice to the archers who now aimed in her direction, awaiting orders to kill her.

"Would you kill me, Amina, granddaughter of Habe Nohi? Would you cut me down like a stray animal on open ground when all I offer you is freedom from the stranger, from the coward who has taken you captive?"

She paused and waited for a command to sound from within the village walls, for arrows to fly towards her in obedience to such a command.

She felt fear. But she suppressed it. She steadied her nerves and narrowed her eyes. This was her purpose - to free Zazzau and to lead Zazzau. She was ready to die for it if the ancestors willed it so.

At that moment, the village gates opened. There was a scuffle at the gates.

Amina squinted to see what was going on. She smiled, and her heart quickened with the fire of vengeance. There could be no doubt now that this was the will of the ancestors. She was truly favored by them.

Musa, her fellow trainee initiate, emerged from the gates, grabbing a fearful looking Habe Nikitau by the shoulder. Two other initiates emerged as well behind him, and shoved Habe Nikitau towards Amina.

Habe Nikitau advanced hesitantly towards Amina. He had been stripped of his royal babban rigga, dressed in a warrior dashiki, and armed with the royal sword and shield.

As Habe Nikitau walked towards his daughter, Musa declared in a loud voice for all to hear as they were all watching through the crevices in the fence.

"Zazzau's Habes have always been honorable, and courageous men. The daughter of one of such honorable Habes stands before us now, offering her people freedom from tyranny.

We, the people of Zazzau remain ready to serve our new Habe, Nikitau and, our conqueror Etsu Tsudi. But we cannot ignore this opportunity presented to us by one of our own, by one of royal blood.

Therefore, we the people accept Amina's challenge to fight our Habe. Should he win, we shall remain loyal subjects of Etsu Tsudi. But should he lose..."

Musa allowed his words to trail off. The message was clear.

Amina's smile turned to a deep frown as she looked into the fearful eyes of her advancing father.

She recalled memories of this man raping her mother. She recalled memories of his drunken, lazy self-demeaning her mother.

How dare this lazy ape sit on a Zazzau throne and call himself Habe? How dare he sell the soul of Zazzau to a stranger for his own personal gain?

As these memories and thoughts clouded her mind, she forced all recognition of him as her father out of her mind. This man is not my father, she told herself. He is a traitor to Zazzau and has therefore been rejected by our ancestors. He must die so that Zazzau can be free. He must die so my mother can deliver her child in peace and live out the rest of her days in freedom.

Nikitau now stood a few feet away from his daughter. He glanced at the slain body of Madaki Ahmed and trembled in fear. "So, Baba. The time of reckoning is upon us. Where do we go from here?" asked Amina.

Nikitau's voice was a shaky whisper.

"Amina, my daughter. Our people say to heed the words of an elder is to drink from an everlasting fountain of youth. Please heed my words. I am still your father, and I care about you. I'm certain we can work out an arrangement. I can speak to Etsu Tsudi on your behalf. I am sure..."

Nikitau's words ended abruptly as did his life.

AMINA MAKING OF A QUEEN

Amina moved with the speed of a viper and slit his throat faster than he could reach up to block the attack. Blood filled his mouth, and he began to choke on it. It poured down from his neck as he clutched his shattered gullet in a feeble, desperate attempt to hold on to life.

Amina dropped the bloodied dagger. She had already begun marching towards the village when her father's body collapsed behind her, beside the corpse of Madaki Ahmed.

The gates of Zazzau flew open. Shouts of joy filled the air as Zazzau villagers, led by Musa and Princess Bakwa, flooded the dusty arena and raced towards Amina.

Amina broke into a wide smile with tears of joy streaming down her face. She broke into a run towards her overwhelmed mother, towards her joyous people. When she reached her mother, she embraced her. They both fell on their knees, weeping tears of joy and relief. Her emotional reunion with her mother was short-lived as she was quickly lifted high by a sea of ecstatic villagers. The Zazzau people chanted in unison:

"Amina! Amina! Amina! She is a woman greater than any man."

"Princess Amina has delivered us from our misery. She will save us from the Nupe. She will restore our glory. She will lead us into victory," declared Musa.

The people lifted her higher and responded with the chant: *"Amina! Amina! Amina! She is a woman greater than a man."*

Amina's heart swelled with pride, and her face was now awash with tears. She resolved in her heart that she would make Zazzau a force to reckon with as far as the Songhai empire in the west, and the Mediterranean Sea in the east.

Amina resolved that never again would Zazzau be caught off-guard. She would protect Zazzau and crush its enemies with an offensive strategy. She would begin her offense with vengeance on the Nupe dog who had murdered thousands of her people and taken thousands more captive.

AUTHOR'S NOTE

I always knew I would be a writer. Growing up in Nigeria, I was fascinated by the cultural cauldron of the Hausa, Igbo, and Yoruba tribes living together as one nation with over 250 smaller ethnic groups.

Each community cherished elegant legends of historical heroes - inspiring stories of courage, triumph and adventure. I discovered that similar cultural heroes were celebrated in other communities across the vast continent of Africa. Disappointingly, however, these African icons were hardly known on the global stage.

This book is about Queen Amina of Zazzau, a sixteenth century West African legend. But it represents something even larger - it is a foray via fiction into the rich world of African history and culture.

Fourteenth century Emperor Mansa Musa of Mali is considered one of the richest men in history. He was so rich that he inadvertently devalued metal for a decade in Mecca when he generously gave away lots of gold during one visit.

Eighteenth century King Jaja was a rich, oil merchant that created wealth in Opobo, Nigeria, and opposed British monopoly.

Sixteenth century Queen Nzingha of Angola opposed Portuguese slave traders and forced the invaders to accept her terms.

These are just a few stories of powerful African heroes whose fascinating stories must be told.

So, I am thrilled to share a side of Africa that is seldom acknowledged. I invite you to join me on a journey that explores the power, the fortitude, and the cultural wealth of the legends who emerged from this continent aptly referred to as "The Home of Human Civilization."

AUTHOR'S NOTE

I always knew I would be a writer. Growing up in Nigeria, I was fascinated by the cultural cauldron of the Hausa, Igbo, and Yoruba tribes living together as one nation with over 250 smaller ethnic groups.

Each community cherished elegant legends of historical heroes - inspiring stories of courage, triumph and adventure. I discovered that similar cultural heroes were celebrated in other communities across the vast continent of Africa. Disappointingly, however, these African icons were hardly known on the global stage.

This book is about Queen Amina of Zazzau, a sixteenth century West African legend. But it represents something even larger - it is a foray via fiction into the rich world of African history and culture.

Fourteenth century Emperor Mansa Musa of Mali is considered one of the richest men in history. He was so rich that he inadvertently devalued metal for a decade in Mecca when he generously gave away lots of gold during one visit.

Eighteenth century King Jaja was a rich, oil merchant that created wealth in Opobo, Nigeria, and opposed British monopoly. Sixteenth century Queen Nzingha of Angola opposed Portuguese slave traders and forced the invaders to accept her terms.

These are just a few stories of powerful African heroes whose fascinating stories must be told.

So, I am thrilled to share a side of Africa that is seldom acknowledged. I invite you to join me on a journey that explores the power, the fortitude, and the cultural wealth of the legends who emerged from this continent aptly referred to as "The Home of Human Civilization."

ACKNOWLEDGEMENTS

My dear wife, Toyin. Without your encouragement, love and support, this book would not have been written. Thank you for being you.

Feolu and Simi, my wonderful sons. Thank you for encouraging me to finish the book, for reading excerpts and exclaiming: "Wow!"

Mom, thank you for a firm foundation, and for buying me a treasure trove of novels that instilled in me a love for reading and writing as a kid.

Dad, and my brothers - Dolapo, Abimbola and, Bukola. Thank you for being such strong role models in my life's journey.

Rotimi Odeniran, my man, you are a true friend. Thank you for being the first beta reader outside my family.

Charlene da Silva, my editor. I appreciate your thoroughness, insights, and the extra boost of confidence.

Samia Javed, my maps illustrator. Your creativity and attention to detail was exactly what I needed.

Martin CS, my cover designer. You are a master of your craft.